Colors in the Dreamweaver's Loom

Colors in the Dreamweaver's Loom

Beth Hilgartner

Houghton Mifflin Company
Boston   1989

Library of Congress Cataloging-in-Publication Data

Hilgartner, Beth.
  Colors in the dreamweaver's loom / by Beth Hilgartner.
      p. cm.
  Summary: Distraught over her father's death, Zan wanders into the
forest and into a fantasy world where she becomes involved in the
Orathi's fight to save their homeland from invaders.
  ISBN 0-395-50214-4
  [1. Fantasy.]   I. Title.
PZ7.H5474Co   1989   89–1815
[Fic] — dc 19   CIP
                          AC

Printed in the United States of America

P 10 9 8 7 6 5 4 3 2 1

for Marjorie

A Note on the Language

In the Senathii, references to a specific member of one of the peoples (that is, Orathi, Vemathi, etc.) use a form of the name which indicates the gender of the person in question. For example, a desert woman is called a Khedath*eh* (-eh being the feminine ending); a man is called a Khedath*en* (-en being the masculine form). If the gender of the individual is unknown, the neuter form, Khedath, is used. The -i ending is plural.

Colors in the Dreamweaver's Loom

ONE

The car flew down the interstate, the open window in back setting up a deafening throb of air. Zan tried to retreat into mindlessness, into the automatic precision that kept the car on the road. The noise from the window was supposed to help. It didn't. She could still picture Rolly's raised eyebrows, hear his urbane tone: "Now Alexandra, won't it wait until after the Press has your statement?" Rolly always said "press" with a capital *P*. "They promised they wouldn't be long if we'd cooperate."

"*Cooperate?*" The shell around her emotions had cracked, freeing a scalding rush of fury. "Your journalistic jackals can paw over Dad's body, but they can't have me!" She had stormed out, slamming the door on his protests: one simply doesn't treat the Press in such a cavalier manner — not when a good (or bad) review can make such a difference. But Zan had been past caring. Her anger had lasted long enough to get her into the elderly Volvo, and she had roared out of the driveway before her temper could cool. Carried by her rage, she had made her way to the interstate and headed south.

As the cool green Vermont countryside streamed by, Zan had let go of the anger. She drove on, dry-eyed. After a while she clicked the radio on: some jazz; then, a little later, the news. She wasn't really listening, but suddenly the announcer's voice intruded. "Pulitzer Prize–winning author Alister Scarsdale is dead at the age of forty-one. The English-born author of *Meeker Street* and *The Obdurate Season* was vacationing in Vermont when he suffered a fatal heart attack —"

Zan killed the radio. She didn't want to hear it. She knew he was dead; she had known from the moment his inert form was wheeled into the hospital. But no child is ever ready for the death of a parent. Her father had been part of her life from before she could remember. She couldn't accept that he was dead. Even when she had stood looking down at his body, it wasn't real. It was too much like a dream — like many dreams. Only this time she wouldn't waken to his sarcastic call: "I suppose you're planning to sleep all day?"

Her hands tightened on the steering wheel. He was dead. *Dead,* damn it! She ought to be sad. Why did this fury keep surging out of her core? "A temperamental, arrogant, selfish *bastard!*" she said aloud. The road blurred before her; she pulled over and stopped. She rested her head against one arm while her thin frame shook with her racking grief.

It was the first time she'd been able to cry for him at all. Even now she wasn't sure whether she was crying for him or for herself, couldn't tell whether her tears were from grief for a life snuffed out untimely or from anger at herself for all the things unsaid. There were a thousand things she hadn't said, a thousand times she'd bitten back reproaches to keep peace. With an upwelling of bitter tears, she remembered the time he had told Rolly that the best thing about Zan was that she knew how not to be a nuisance. That was pretty thin praise; but it was praise, and because she had so desperately wanted his approval, she had stifled her complaints. She had never told him how much she resented him for dragging her all over Europe and the States in the wake of his elusive muse, for preventing her from having a home and friends her own age. She had never told him how much she resented him for stealing her childhood. She had kept silent, afraid that if she began with reproaches, he would retaliate by telling her things she couldn't bear to hear: that he had never expected to be saddled with a toddler when his wife of three years was killed in an accident; that in fact he wished Zan had never been born.

She had never told him any of this — coward! — and now it was too late. She had been afraid; she had hoped, like a child, that things would improve, that Dad would change, that he would somehow — suddenly, miraculously — understand what she needed without being told. She was planning to enter Harvard in the fall. She had believed that with four years in the same place she would be able, finally, to come to terms with him. Now . . . now she would have to come to terms without him.

Zan drew a shuddering deep breath. The slow exhalation was pocked by a couple of hiccupping gulps, but control was slowly returning. After a while she dug about in the glove compartment in search of a tissue. She blew her nose and mopped her eyes. If she stayed here too long, a trooper might stop, and she dreaded having to explain. She reached for the ignition key.

She froze the motion before she turned the key. Instead, she got out of the car. Around her the mountains brooded, hunching their green shoulders. The air smelled of forest, of peace. She could see the thin trail of a train track, then a muddy twist of the Winooski, but across the highway the woods looked like another world. They were untouched, impossibly distant, utterly inaccessible: heaven. She contrasted the mountains with the thought of the press, gathered even now with her father's agent, Rolly Castleman, collecting scraps of Alister Scarsdale's life for their faceless readers. If the thought of explaining herself to a single trooper was daunting, acting normal for a pack of reporters was terrifying.

Zan walked to the guardrail and sat down on it. The afternoon was quiet except for the chirrup of insects in the grass. There were no traffic noises, no human sounds at all. Acting on an impulse she did not stop to analyze, Zan returned to the car, took her Windbreaker out of the back seat, and closed the door slowly. She walked around the car to the driver's side, then, looking back down the empty track of highway, she crossed it. On the far side there was a short, steep slope leading down to a shaded dell. The woods began beyond a little brook and stretched away forever. For a moment Zan hesitated, as if some saner part of herself were trying to reconsider. Then, with a defiant lift of her chin, she stepped over the railing. She went down the embankment without looking back.

It was steeper than it looked. She slid the last ten feet, squelched through a marshy spot, and hopped over the brook. As she moved onto drier ground, into the shadow of the trees, the silence of the woods swallowed her.

TWO

Zan walked. It took some effort to stay upright; ferny undergrowth hid downed limbs and the unevenness of the ground. The going was rough, and soon, even in the cool green shade of the forest, she was too warm. She was plagued by mosquitoes. Her steps slowed, finally stopping like a run-down clock. Reason tried to reassert itself. She looked over her shoulder at the trampled ferns in her wake. She was being stupid. She would go back, back to her car, the cottage, Rolly — and the reporters. Vividly, her mind presented an image of ants swarming around spilled ice cream on the sidewalk. No; she thrust the thought away with disgust. No reporters. Ignoring the cool, reasonable thought that told her to go back before she got lost, she went on.

Gradually the woods changed. The trees grew larger, the shade deeper, the ferns sparser. The land rose under her feet; Zan climbed, heedless. After a particularly steep stretch, she sat down to rest. Her father's face rose in her mind. Her emotions uncoiled suddenly and grief surged up. Zan flung herself flat on the ground and gave herself up to tears. She cried herself to sleep.

The cold woke her. The sun had slipped behind the shoulder of the hill and the forest was in murky shadow. Zan sat up. She huddled into her Windbreaker. Abruptly she realized she had only the vaguest notion of the way she had come. The memory of the woods, stretching limitlessly out along the interstate, filled her mind's eye. She imagined herself wandering in futile spirals until she dropped. Panic leered at her, made her breathless. She told herself that already people would be searching for her, but reason was a feeble defense against fear. The feelings she had kept in such tight control rebelled. She leapt to her feet and began to run headlong down the hill. She clipped a tree with one shoulder; it threw her off balance and her knee buckled. She fell, jouncing and rolling down the steep slope. She struck another tree and her world exploded into stars.

Hearing returned first, hearing and pain. Her whole body ached. Zan lay still, listening to the faint twitter of birds. Slowly she realized there was light on the other side of her eyelids. She tried opening them and shut them hurriedly. The world lurched, and the drummer in her skull beat a thundering rhythm. But it was light — not dawn, morning. After a few minutes she tried again. This time she had better success. With care she could even focus on the ground before her, on the delicate moss forests beneath her nose, on her own scratched hand, six inches away; then, greatly daring, she moved her gaze to the pair of beaded leather shoes beyond her hand. There were feet in the shoes. She started up in surprise, only to drop back to the moss with a groan as dizziness flooded her skull. She must be imagining things — or dreaming. That was it. She would just lie here, quite still, until she really woke up.

Then she felt a gentle touch on her shoulder. A face was leaning over her, a thin, sharp-chinned face with wide brown eyes and a frown of concern. As the face began to move in sickening circles, Zan shut her eyes again.

"Go away," she muttered. "You're a dream."

But the hand didn't leave her shoulder, so after a while, gingerly, Zan rolled over and sat up. It took several moments, with her eyes shut and her head resting on her knees, before the world stopped whirling. Finally she opened her eyes and studied the dream that wouldn't go away. It was a girl, fine-boned and delicate, with an untidy tangle of curly brown hair. She was dressed very oddly, in a short tunic of rough-looking material over a pair of suede trousers. The girl studied Zan with her head cocked to one side like a sparrow, smiling tentatively. Zan smiled back.

"Well, I guess you aren't a dream," Zan said at last. "I don't suppose you could show me how to get back to the highway?"

A puzzled frown clouded the bright eyes.

"Interstate 89," Zan added, struggling to keep the impatience out of her voice.

The girl's puzzlement deepened.

Zan suppressed a sigh. Though the girl looked eleven or

twelve, she must be younger than that to be so perplexed. Zan tried a reassuring tone. "It's okay. I'm Zan and I'm lost. Maybe your parents can help me."

The girl took Zan's hand and tugged gently.

"You want me to come with you? Well, okay, I'll try. I don't feel too good, though." Zan struggled to her feet and took a step or two. "God, I'm all bruises," she muttered. But her legs worked. She limped along beside the strange girl. Suddenly the girl stopped, her face breaking into a smile. She pursed her lips and trilled a birdcall. There was an answering birdcall and a boy stepped into view. He was dressed like the girl, but he held a bow and, on his back, a quiver of arrows. *Playing Indians*, Zan thought with a twinge of envy over the care someone had taken with their costumes. The boy came over to her, staring especially at her red hair, then said something she didn't understand.

"I beg your pardon," she said, before the truth dawned on her. He wasn't speaking a language she recognized, and she'd learned a number of them trailing through Europe after her father.

The boy said something else. "I don't understand you," she said, her voice rising. "Don't you speak English?"

He turned to the girl and spoke sharply. She shrugged and gestured rapidly. He shook his head, returning her shrug. Then he turned back to Zan and laid his right hand on his chest. "Karivet." Then he pointed to the girl. "Iobeh."

Zan pointed to herself, playing along. "Zan."

His eyebrows rose and he made a small motion as though

to step back. " 'Tsan," he repeated, then gestured with his head. Iobeh tugged on Zan's hand and they started walking again in the direction Karivet had indicated.

"If you two are playing a joke on me," Zan said, "I hope your parents flay you."

Iobeh turned to her, but Zan just shrugged. "Never mind."

They walked for a long while. Zan had to stop to rest several times. Each time, Iobeh smiled and patted Zan's shoulder. Zan found the contact oddly comforting. As she struggled over the rough terrain, she alternated between a detached sort of lightheadedness and an insistent, thudding headache. She did not have much attention to spare for her surroundings. The whole situation seemed an elaborate practical joke.

When they came out of the trees into sunlight, Zan halted, blinking in the brightness. They were on the side of a gentle hill that sloped down to a quiet valley with a river running through it. There were goats and sheep in the meadow, and farther away, between the river and the forest, an orderly cluster of small stone houses with thatched roofs. Beyond the houses, on the far side of the river, the forest began again.

"Dear God," Zan whispered, her eyes wide as panic swooped up again. She spun around, desperately looking for escape, for anything that offered a hope of normality. The sudden movement was too much for her. There was a fierce roaring in her ears and her sight began to dim at the edges. She sat down, putting her head between her knees.

The dizziness took a long time to subside. Zan felt Iobeh's hand on her shoulder; at first she wanted to shake it off, but the very idea of movement made her stomach heave. After several minutes she began to feel oddly calm, as though there were some external soothing influence. Part of her resisted it, but gradually she grew calmer. When the world had ceased spinning, she raised her head and got stiffly to her feet. Iobeh took her hand, and Karivet came to Zan's other side and took hold of her elbow. With both of them steadying her, they made their way into the village.

The main thoroughfare led past small courtyards, each with a well at its center and bordered on three sides by houses. Orderly garden plots, only beginning to show signs of the vegetables they would bear, separated the houses. People, all dressed like Iobeh and Karivet, worked in the gardens or wandered about the squares. Most of them stopped their work to gawk at Zan, and a few stood in their doorways, but no one spoke.

The track ran through the village toward the river, then turned parallel to the river. Karivet and Iobeh guided Zan along it, through an orchard, until they reached a house set apart from the rest of the village. Karivet left them by the gate, went up the flagged path to the door, and knocked loudly. After several moments the door opened. Zan saw a tiny old woman framed by the doorway. She and Karivet spoke together softly and hurriedly. Finally she motioned them all inside.

The main room of the cottage was dominated by a large loom. Zan stared at the work on the loom; it seemed so out of character for these homespun keepers of goats and sheep. The cloth was beautiful, with clear, bright blues, soft grays,

11

and a fine texture. The pattern was subtle, drawing the eye into it. Zan kept trying comparisons in her mind without finding any to fit. Suddenly she realized the others were all looking at her.

"I'm sorry." Gesturing to the loom, she added, "It's very beautiful."

The old woman cocked her head curiously, then smiled at Zan. She waved at the loom, then pointed to Zan with a lift to her eyebrows.

"Do *I* weave?" Zan asked, surprised. "No — but I wish I could." She remembered to shake her head "no" when the others looked at her blankly.

The old woman shrugged. " 'Tsan," she said with a side-long glance at Karivet.

Zan nodded.

"Eikoheh Simirandeh," she said, indicating herself.

Zan repeated the name hesitantly; the woman smiled. Then she turned to the others, spoke, and made rapid shoo-ing motions. While Iobeh and Karivet moved into the far end of the room, Eikoheh took Zan by the arm, steered her to the window, and began examining the nylon fabric of her Windbreaker. Zan took it off and gave it to her, watching the old woman's surprise and excitement at the elasticized wrists and the zipper. Eikoheh then scrutinized the striped oxford cloth of Zan's shirt.

Meanwhile Zan studied her surroundings. The loom stood between two windows glazed with heavy, bubble-pocked glass that distorted the view of the vegetable plot beyond but admitted adequate light for working. Beyond the loom was a spinning wheel, two heavy wooden chests piled high with skeins of dyed yarn, and several bales of wool carefully stacked against the wall. The far wall of the cottage, opposite the two windows, was taken up by the hearth, where a sullen fire glowered under an iron kettle set on a metal tripod. There was neither table nor chairs, except the hard wooden bench in front of the loom. As Zan's tired brain registered the lack of chairs, she saw that Iobeh was gathering cushions and small rugs into four piles. Karivet had taken an earthenware pitcher and four cups from the shelves beside the hearth and was setting them on the floor among Iobeh's piles. That done, he went back to the shelves for more dishes. Above the kitchen half of the main room was a loft, reached by ladderlike stairs. Hung from the beams were ropes of onions, bundles of dried herbs, and something that looked as though it might be dried meat. A number of implements were arranged with care near the hearth. Two massive wooden bins flanked the open back door, through which Zan could see the curved rim of a well.

As the weaver bent down to examine the worn corduroy of Zan's trousers, the unreality of the situation suddenly made itself felt. Zan shook her head. "This is stupid. It can't be happening. I must be completely crazy. Or it's a dream — a *weird* dream." She hunched her shoulders and hugged herself. She looked at Eikoheh, who was watching Zan warily. "You are delusions — all of you! And I want to wake up."

Eikoheh studied her for a moment; then, as Karivet called out to her, she led Zan to a pile of cushions. Before she let her sit, Eikoheh patted the top of the pile.

"*Rekas*," she said. "*E barenda ho rekas.*" Language lessons had begun.

The delusions didn't go away; the food smelled good. With a mental shrug at the absurdity of it all, Zan ate what they served. Throughout the meal, Eikoheh continued the language lesson; she insisted that Zan ask for the things she wanted to eat by name. The main part of the meal consisted of the contents of the kettle, a concoction of grains, vegetables, and fish rather like a cross between porridge and stew; Eikoheh called it *kemess.* They ate from wooden bowls. Zan mimicked the way they balanced the bowls on their knees and held their heavy-handled, wide-bowled spoons. With the stew there was a white, crumbly, strong-smelling cheese Zan suspected had come from a goat, and a sweet, nutty flat bread. To drink, there was a pitcher of *ifenn,* a sharp-flavored, pale golden liquid that left a sweet aftertaste.

The food restored Zan; she began to feel less dizzy, less remote, more able to fall in with whatever it was her delusions wanted. Throughout the meal, Eikoheh insisted Zan ask for things, prompting her and correcting her pronunciation. Though she felt like a parrot, by the time they were finished Zan was requesting food with (she supposed) the equivalents of pleases and thank-yous. Eikoheh beamed. Even Karivet began to look a little less doubtful, while Iobeh all but purred.

After the meal there was another muttered council between the old woman and the boy. Zan did what they bade, as well as she could make out, though her sense of unreality

14

did not lessen. Eikoheh showed her guest to a pallet — a rush mat covered by thick, soft furs — in the sleeping loft, and Zan lay down. Perhaps if she went back to sleep, she would wake up in the real world.

It didn't work. She woke late in the afternoon in the loft of the weaver's cottage, feeling much better. She was full of questions, but had no way to ask them. So what if this was a dream or a delusion? It seemed real enough. Besides, without the language, it was impossible for her to get any more information than what she could gather with her senses. She climbed down the ladder, resolved to learn to communicate as quickly as possible. The others greeted her warmly; they seemed aware of the shift in her attitude and welcomed it.

Eventually it was agreed that Zan would stay with the weaver rather than with Iobeh and Karivet. Zan was a little surprised to discover the children did not live in the cottage. With a wry inward smile, she guessed they must have brought her to the village expert on weird strangers. The weaver's first project was to make clothing for Zan. By dint of many gestures and facial expressions, she indicated that it would be unwise, even unsafe, for Zan to go into the village until she was able to talk with the people. Zan doubted it could be that dangerous, but she couldn't exactly discuss it.

Zan worked diligently at the language. Almost the first thing she worked out to say was "Please take me home." Eikoheh tried gently to explain, but Zan was beyond listening. She just repeated her phrase, over and over, while her tears streamed unchecked. Finally, one day Karivet and Iobeh took her back into the forest, back to the place where they had found her, to show her that there was nothing there. Zan insisted they search a long way in the dense forest before she finally collapsed, from weariness and despair, and wept bitterly. She probably would have cried herself to sleep, but Iobeh and Karivet made her get up after a while, and took her back to the weaver's cottage. Zan managed an outward calm, but inside she kept telling herself, with an insistence born of fear, that this was a dream, that she would have to wake up soon.

As time passed and her command of the language grew, her denial began to fade gently into a kind of aching acceptance. The days weren't the hardest thing she faced, for then she was kept busy. Karivet helped her with the language, and Eikoheh found an endless round of tasks and chores for her. But the nights were a different story. As soon as the lamps were blown out, Zan was overwhelmed with loneliness, and with loss. Her father's face intruded in her dreams or in that mindless span between wakefulness and sleep, and she would find herself stifling sobs. She was acutely conscious of the closeness of the weaver's cottage, but she lacked the words to explain, or to seek comfort. Instead she grimly endured the nights, waiting for daylight — and the presence of the children — to distract her.

As the days passed, Zan became aware of the fact that Iobeh sat silently by while Karivet helped her with the language. Iobeh never spoke. At first Zan thought she was just shy, then she began to wonder whether there was something wrong with her. When she finally managed to ask Eikoheh about it, the old woman looked at her sharply.

16

"Iobeh speaks with the heart. Can you not hear her?"

Zan struggled to make sense of the answer. "Speaks with the *what?*" she asked. The word Eikoheh had used was unfamiliar.

"The heart," the old woman repeated, laying an open hand on her own breastbone. "Do you not hear her?"

Zan frowned. "Not — *words,*" she said at last.

"The heart does not need words."

Zan chewed her lip as she tried to frame her next question. "Then how does she tell her . . . her . . . story?"

The old woman's serious expression lightened. "For that you must learn the speech of her hands."

"Speech of her" — Zan pointed at her own palm — "*hands?*" Then she remembered Iobeh's rapid, graceful hand gestures. "Oh! I see."

Eikoheh nodded and went back to her weaving.

Over the course of the next few weeks, Eikoheh taught Zan many things. By the end of the third week, Zan had picked up enough of the language — the Senathii, "the speech of the peoples" — to understand simple conversations, as long as people spoke slowly. She learned that her name, as Karivet pronounced it, meant something like "stranger." *Utsan,* not-common, strange: 'Tsan. It must have seemed an appropriate name to her hosts, she thought wryly.

Besides the Senathii, Zan learned useful household things. She learned how to drop the wooden bucket down the well so that it filled with water and sank instead of bobbing frustratingly on the surface. She learned how to make *kemess* and the sweet flat bread they ate. She learned how to milk

17

the goats — and how hard they were to catch when they got loose in the vegetable garden. The weaver taught her how to card and spin wool. Even though she got quite adept at spinning fine, even thread, Eikoheh adamantly refused to permit Zan to try her hand at the loom.

"To weave is to lay your life in the pattern," Eikoheh told her. "You are not ready for that."

"How? I don't understand," Zan replied.

"No, you don't. But it is so."

Zan fought back a sigh. There was much that Eikoheh dismissed by saying simply "It is so."

One afternoon Iobeh came alone. She signed to Eikoheh, who explained that Karivet had gone honey-gathering, something he liked to do by himself. Iobeh looked a little wistful. Zan suddenly felt sorry for her; it must be lonely to be unable to talk to others.

"Iobeh," she said suddenly, "will you teach me the speech of your hands?"

A smile made Iobeh's face radiant. She nodded.

"How many people understand your hand-speech?"

Iobeh held up two fingers.

"You can talk only to Eikoheh and Karivet?" Zan demanded, then frowned, puzzled. "But what about your —" She paused; she couldn't remember the word for parents, so had to settle for something less precise. "What about your kin?"

Iobeh's smile vanished, but Eikoheh answered for her. "She and Karivet have no kin. When they were very small, there was fever in the village. Many people died — including their parents."

"Then where do they live, Eikoheh? Who takes care of them?"

The old woman shrugged. "They live in what was their parents' house. People in the village give them food, and Karivet hunts. It's not an easy life, but they do not complain."

Zan shook her head. The arrangement seemed terribly loose, but it appeared to work; the children were well fed and clothed. She returned to her original question. "Iobeh, you can talk only to Eikoheh and Karivet?" she asked, and at the girl's nod added, "But that's *awful!*"

Iobeh shrugged, then, with a little smile, pointed to Zan and held up three fingers.

"Yes, I will make a third — but it will take time."

Iobeh nodded.

"Iobeh, how many summers have you?"

She held up ten fingers, then two.

"And Karivet?"

She repeated the gesture.

"You're, you're —" Zan stopped when she realized she didn't know the word for twins. "You *are* brother and sister, yes?"

Iobeh nodded.

"Is it common among your people to have two children with the same number of summers?"

Iobeh smiled and shook her head.

Eikoheh looked up from her weaving and chuckled. "You are getting cleverer, 'Tsan. The word is *imadi*, and they are very rare. Often one or both of the twins have *yskar-ekabi*. They are called gifts, but are rather burdens. People fear *yskar-ekabi*, and fear makes them cruel."

Ekabi — Zan knew that; it meant "gifts." "Eikoheh, what is *yskar*?"

The old woman shrugged. "That's a hard one. Your *yskar* is what leaps at beauty; it is the flame that burns within the lamp of your body; it is that which makes you yourself. Surely your people have a word for it?"

Zan puzzled over it. Mind? Personality? Virtue? None of them seemed quite right. "Is it that which weaves words together before I put them on my lips?" she asked.

"No. It is deeper than that. Anyone who is whole and well can think, but it is the *yskar* that makes them *your* thoughts."

"Spirit," Zan said aloud, finally. Eikoheh looked up questioningly. "I understand — at least, I hope so. I haven't any more words to guess with. Can you explain spirit-gifts to me? Do Iobeh and Karivet have them?"

"Explain them? No. They are; that is enough. Iobeh might show you hers one day, and Karivet must speak for himself, if he chooses. I told you this so that you will understand the other villagers. They are wary of the twins, and sometimes unkind. That is all." She picked up the shuttle and sent it flying through the warp.

For a moment Zan merely listened to the rhythmic sounds of Eikoheh's handiwork. Suddenly she looked up and caught Iobeh's anxious expression. With a smile, Zan touched her hand. "I'm not afraid of you, Iobeh, if that is what makes you frown. You are kind and good, and I —" She shrugged. "I am *utsan;* I don't know enough to be afraid."

Without pausing in her weaving, Eikoheh said, "*Utsan*eh. *Utsan* is a thing."

Zan smiled wryly at Iobeh. "*Utsaneh*, then. But in any case, I am not afraid."

Iobeh gave Zan an impulsive hug. Then she took Zan's hand and tugged. Zan got up and went with her. Eikoheh watched them go but said nothing.

It was a glorious afternoon, full of warm green smells and the lazy drone of bees. Iobeh took Zan into the orchard and sat down beneath an apple tree. Zan joined her, but when she would have spoken, Iobeh touched her fingers to Zan's lips and shook her head. Then she folded her hands in her lap, closed her eyes, and bowed her head. She sat that way for several minutes, then slowly she raised her head and held out one hand. To Zan's utter amazement, a song sparrow lighted on Iobeh's outstretched finger. Iobeh cupped the bird in her hand and whistled to it. It trilled. Iobeh whistled encouragingly. The little bird tilted back its head and poured out its song. Zan watched and listened, delighted. After a time Iobeh tossed the bird back into the air and watched it dwindle in the distance.

"Iobeh," Zan said, her voice full of wonder, "what a precious Gift you have. Do you speak with your heart to the birds?"

Iobeh looked up, surprised, then nodded. Suddenly her eyes brimmed with tears. Zan put her arms around the girl, felt her confusion, her sadness. She struggled to put into words what she thought was bothering Iobeh.

"The birds understand. They know enough not to fear you, but people don't. Is that it?"

Against her shoulder, Iobeh nodded vigorously.

"Well, *I'm* not afraid of your Gift. Maybe we can teach others not to be."

For a long moment they sat together, content in the silence. Then, at last, Iobeh got to her feet, gesturing toward Eikoheh's house.

Zan sighed. "You're right," she conceded, getting up. "It must be nearly time for supper."

THREE

The crescent moon swelled to full; the time drifted by as softly as apple blossoms. Zan's misery eased a little. Her nights were less often troubled by loneliness and weeping, though thinking of her father still brought tears to her eyes. It wasn't that she missed him, exactly, for he had been difficult and demanding, but there was so much left unsaid — by her, and she suspected by him — which would never now be resolved. It made her ache inside, but she was growing used to that pain, and there was a great deal to distract her. Karivet and Iobeh worked hard to teach Zan both their sign language and the Senathii. She progressed steadily, though not as quickly as she would have liked.

They taught her other things as well, sharing with her bits of the history of their people, the Orathi: the people of the forest. Karivet explained that they had not always lived in villages. Once, not so long ago, all the Orathi had dwelt in trees, on platforms sealed from the wind by animal skins. It sounded uncomfortable to Zan, and she said so. Iobeh smiled and nodded, but Karivet went to some trouble to make her understand that not all the Orathi had abandoned the old ways, that in fact many, if not most, still lived deep within the forest, scorning the keeping of flocks and building of stone shelters. It all sounded peculiar to Zan, but Karivet's lessons helped to pass the time.

Despite the distractions provided by the twins, time often seemed like the oil level in one of Eikoheh's lamps; it never changed while one watched, despite the clear, steady flame. Since Zan only went outside with the twins, and never into the village, she began to feel confined. Eikoheh understood her frustration, but counseled caution.

"'Tsan," she said, shaking her head, "the villagers are very shy, wary of strangers. You must be patient with them."

"Yes, yes," Zan retorted, wiping the dinner dishes with unnecessary energy. "But how can they grow used to me if they never even see me? I haven't seen anyone but you and the twins since the first day I came. I will seem as strange to them a season from now, unless —" She broke off, tangled in the language. "If you do not send the shuttle through the warp, the weaving does not grow, no matter how long you sit at the loom."

"True," the old woman conceded. "But if the shuttle carries no thread, the work is pointless. You must be able to speak with them, 'Tsan."

Zan recognized Eikoheh's expression; she took the hint and let the subject drop. She finished the dishes and did a little spinning, hoping the work would help her find patience.

Zan did not sleep well that night. Her dreams left her feeling as though she had been handed a truth she was too dense to interpret. In the one she remembered best, she was desperately searching the crowded, anonymous reaches of some vast airport. Despair lurked like a predator. As her search became more frantic, she found she could not even remember what she sought. Finally she woke, weeping with desolation. Grimly conscious of the cottage's close quarters, Zan stifled her noise in the sleeping furs. When at last she stopped crying, it still took her a long time to fall asleep again; mercifully, the rest of the night was dreamless.

The next morning she woke later than usual. To her surprise, it was Karivet who sat beside the hearth stirring the breakfast porridge. Neither his twin nor the weaver was there.

"Are you hungry?" he asked, filling her bowl.

"Yes, thank you. Where is Eikoheh — and Iobeh?"

He gave her the bowl and a small jar of wild honey. "They've gone to market. I said I'd wait for you. You slept a long time."

"I didn't sleep well. I had bad —" She stopped. She didn't know the word for dreams. "My sleep was troubled."

He filled his own dish, moved away from the hearth, and sat down facing her. "Bad what?" he asked after a moment.

Zan ran a hand through her hair. "I don't know the word. The — the stories your thoughts tell while you sleep."

"The word is *simi*, but what do you mean, *bad* ones?

Dreams are patterns of the truth, neither good nor bad."

He sounded stiff, and Zan wondered whether she had offended him. She struggled to clarify. "Among my people, it is not uncommon for dreams to be a . . . a sign of an . . . inward trouble. There may be truth in them, but when they draw the trouble to the surface, we call them 'bad' dreams."

He toyed with his spoon as he considered her words. "Would you . . ." he began hesitantly. "Would you tell me what you dreamed, 'Tsan?"

"I don't really remember," she hedged. She didn't see how she could explain an airport to him, and she wasn't sure she wanted to try. His expression was faintly disapproving. It made her suddenly uncomfortable. "Why do you care, anyway?" she demanded. "Why should it matter what I dream?"

He set his bowl down abruptly and fixed her with a level gaze. "You need not tell me if you do not wish to. I asked because among my people dreams are rare. Spirit-gifts are often heralded by dreaming. I thought your dreams might give us some hint about why you were sent to us by the wise gods."

"Sent . . . ?" she echoed, shocked. "Look, I wasn't sent here by gods or anyone else!"

"No?" His cool word made Zan flinch. "Then how *did* you come here? And why?"

Zan was silent as gut-wrenching fear slid up her spine. She stared at Karivet for a moment, then looked away, cross-ing her arms tightly. "None of this is real. It's all a dream — or madness brought on by grief." As she spoke, she realized that she no longer believed this. She didn't understand what had happened, or how, but somehow, deep inside her, she knew it was real. She fought the knowledge, shivering.

Karivet sighed heavily. "Iobeh said you had gotten beyond your denial. I see she was mistaken."

"Why should what I think matter?" Zan asked woodenly. "If this is real, it's real, even if I don't believe it."

Karivet thumped one fist into the other palm, irritation clear on his face. " 'Tsan, don't you see? Until we are sure that you believe *this* is *real* — now, here — how can we trust you not to do yourself some harm through carelessness? You cannot go out among others until you understand that your actions have consequences — for you and for us."

"But how do you know it's not a dream?" she asked, though as she spoke, she realized she could no longer retreat into disbelief; the present had grown too immediate.

For a moment she wasn't sure he would answer. He picked up his bowl again, focused his attention on the porridge, and said, "Oh, 'Tsan, I wish I could make you understand! True dreams are vivid, but they are not *real*." He took the spoon out of his bowl and waved it. "You do not *taste* things in a dream. Why do you resist us so?"

Zan set her bowl on the floor and crossed her arms again. "Because I'm frightened," she retorted. "Things like this *don't happen* — so I'm either dreaming or mad."

"Or the world is wider than you imagined," he whispered. A shadow of pain brushed his eyes, which made him seem very much older than his twelve years. Even as his words made her shiver, Zan felt a pang of sympathetic kinship; he did not seem to have been allowed to enjoy childhood either.

"Come on," Karivet said, abruptly breaking the mood. "Help me with the dishes."

They did the dishes without speaking. Zan felt acutely as though she had failed a vital test and would have no other chance to explain her changed attitude, and Karivet seemed to be lost in some dark thoughts of his own. Both of them were startled when the door of the cottage was flung open and Iobeh came in. She and Karivet had a signed conversation, too rapid for Zan to follow, then Iobeh came over, took the cloth out of Zan's hands, and signed slowly: *Come. Don't you wish to see the —— ?*

"Market," Karivet supplied. "Well? Don't you?"

Zan looked from him to his sister and back. "But I thought . . ." she ventured.

He waved his hand. "I yield to Iobeh's judgment. If you wish to go, you shall."

Happy excitement swelled into a smile. "Come on, then!"

In moments the three of them were heading for the open ground on the far side of the village where the market was held. It was a much busier place than Zan had imagined from the twins' offhand attitude. She would never have guessed the town could hold as many people as milled about. When she said as much to Karivet, he shrugged. "They do not all live here. The market draws people who live in the forest — the ones who follow the old ways. You can recognize them often because they wear no woven clothes."

Zan looked at the crowds, trying to tell which of the many people there were villagers and which were not. She was struck suddenly by the remarkable similarity of their physical features. The Orathi were small, fine-boned, and dark; their hair was curly, dark brown or black, and their eyes were brown. Zan, who was tall and had her father's red hair, stuck out like a Percheron in a field of Shetland ponies. It made her feel very conspicuous. The feeling did not fade once they were among the crowds. Wherever they walked, people fell silent and stepped out of their way. Most of them stared at Zan, though a few pretended no interest, just watched her furtively. She remembered Eikoheh's warning that the villagers were unused to strangers, and tried to convince herself that they felt as uncomfortable as she did. She forced herself to stand up straight and to ignore their reactions. Iobeh took her hand and squeezed it. *You will get used to them*, she signed.

Suddenly Karivet stiffened beside her. "Here comes Fafimed," he murmured, looking as though he wanted to say more, but his advice was forestalled by the proximity of its subject.

Fafimed was an old man, spry despite his white hair, but his face was seamed with the tracks of frowns. He studied Zan sourly, sparing only a brief glance for the twins. A corner of Zan's mind noted that he wore a sleeveless tunic of soft deerskin instead of a woven one. "Who are you?" he demanded of her. "You are not a Khedatheh — are you of the Vemathi?"

"I do not know those peoples," Zan replied civilly, trying to keep a tremor out of her voice. Fafimed's glare threatened to unnerve her. "I am a stranger, from a land that knows neither your folk nor your tongue. I speak the Senathii, and that not well, only because of the careful tutoring of Eikoheh and Karivet."

"Oh. Well, if you are under the Dreamweaver's wing, I will not trouble you," the man told her. He turned away, and around her talk began again in nervous whispers.

"Very good," Karivet said. Iobeh squeezed her hand again. "It is fortunate you did not try to claim kinship with the Vemathi."

"Why? Who are they?"

"They are the people of the Vem."

"The what?" Zan cut in.

"Vem. It is like the village, only hundreds of times larger." *City*, Zan's mind supplied as he went on briskly. "You do not look like them at all. Fafimed was testing you; he is a wary one." He turned to his sister. "Where is Eikoheh?"

Iobeh pointed, then led them through the crowd to a place where several stalls of woven goods had been set up. Eikoheh's stall was easy to find; nothing else came even close to her work in quality. Eikoheh looked up from her bargaining and signaled them to wait. As Karivet sat down, Zan caught his eye, noticing for the first time how tired and drawn he looked.

"Karivet, is something wrong?" she asked him.

"Yes — no. I don't know. The market is full of rumors and an ugly temper."

Iobeh gestured, too quickly for Zan to follow, though she caught some words.

"Iobeh says that people are afraid — were afraid even before we came."

Zan nodded but refused to be sidetracked. "I meant is something wrong with you? You look worn."

He hunched one shoulder but did not reply. Moved by a sudden impulse, Zan leaned forward, touched his hand, and caught his eyes.

"Karivet, what do you fear?"

His gaze grew distant, and his voice was flat, without inflection. "I taste ashes on the wind and hear the sound of axes. The Vemathi will fell the forest while the Khedathi wait like falcons for their prey. I fear war, and change, and bloodshed. I fear to speak; I fear to remain silent."

Zan stared at him in amazement; then her lips trembled. He had used Senathii words she knew she had never heard — war, falcons, bloodshed — but she had understood them. She dropped her eyes to their touching hands. Karivet caught her wrist hard and shook it.

" 'Tsan. 'Tsan, what is it?"

She wouldn't look up. "Bloodshed," she whispered. "I've never heard that word before, but I know what it means. I understood you."

He shook harder, forcing her to look up. "What are you talking about? What has bloodshed to do with anything?"

"You said it," Zan said desperately. "Didn't you hear him, Iobeh?"

She nodded, her eyes wide.

"*What* did I say?" he demanded.

Zan repeated it. For a moment he stared blankly; then he covered his face with his hands. "Dear gods."

"I don't understand," Zan said. "What is it? How —"

Eikoheh cut her off, startling her. "We call it *ylhaffend* — to see the wind. It is the rarest of the spirit-gifts, and the hardest to bear. You never told me, Karivet, you could prophesy."

He looked up, anguished. "*I never knew.* I have never done it before!"

Eikoheh's eyes widened. "Ah. It takes a question, then — and Iobeh is mute; she cannot ask it."

I can! Iobeh signed indignantly.

Eikoheh touched her cheek. "I think perhaps the question must be spoken aloud, Iobeh. Try again, 'Tsan: ask him another question."

"Will I ever get home?" she asked.

Karivet's eyes clouded with quick concern and he spread his hands. "Only the pattern on the Weaver's Loom will tell us that, 'Tsan. We will try to make you happy here."

"It didn't work," Zan said to Eikoheh.

"Think. What was different?"

Iobeh tapped Zan's shoulder to get her attention. *You were touching hands before*, she signed.

Zan nodded, then took Karivet's hand and met his eyes. "Will I ever get home, Karivet?"

His gaze went distant. "Home is a place in the heart," he said in that flat, quiet voice.

"Is that yes or no?" she insisted.

"It is both, and neither."

As she released him, his eyes returned to normal. Karivet looked at them all and shivered. "I don't like this," he said. "It cannot be *me* answering. I do not know these things!"

"It is your Gift," Eikoheh told him. "Never doubt it."

"It is not one I want!"

"No one asks for spirit-gifts, Karivet," the old weaver told him quietly. "But you cannot reject that which the gods bestow."

He was silent for a moment. Then he leapt to his feet and raced off through the crowd.

"Wait!" Zan cried, but Iobeh stayed her.

He needs to be alone. He will return, she signed slowly.

Zan's shoulders slumped. "I didn't mean to upset him."

"Nay, you have done him a service," Eikoheh retorted. "Spirit-gifts are hard to bear, but it is much worse to have them unbeknownst; spirit-gifts unacknowledged or denied can fester in one's mind and cause all manner of pain. I have seen it in him." She looked over at Iobeh. "Remember the screaming dreams? Karivet has some talent as a Dreamer, but of late his dreams have caused him more pain than enlightenment. Perhaps this will ease them, now. I have long thought dreaming was not his sole Gift; his presence is too strong. *Ylhaffend.* It fits; it will make him whole. Right now it is hard for him, but believe me, it would be worse later."

"I suppose," Zan agreed doubtfully. "But Eikoheh, what does it all mean? The Vemathi, the City-dwellers — are they really a force to fear? And why?"

"It is dark to me, too, 'Tsan. I —" She broke off and held up one hand. "Listen."

They all heard it, even over the bustle of the marketplace: the shivery call of horns. Slowly the market noises ceased as people fell silent. In the waiting quiet they heard the sound of hoofbeats.

There were four riders, three men and a woman. They were all dressed alike, in gray leather with an intricate pattern worked in gold and red on the breast of the tunics. Two of the men, the ones with the hunting horns, were fair-skinned, with straight black hair. The other two riders had wild blond hair that stood out from their heads like a halo; the hair was nearly white, but their skin was golden and their eyes startlingly dark. They halted their high-strung mounts in the center of the marketplace while the Orathi gathered silently around. Then one of the trumpeters bowed with a flourish, swept the assembled people with cool gray eyes, and began to speak.

"The Lord of the City sends his greetings to the Orathi. He asks that I tell you of our plight so that you may be moved to pity. Of late the City has grown too small for its people, while the Orathi grow too few to people their lands. Our great Lord proposes to take the land east of the Tianneh River" — he gestured toward the river that ran to the west of the little village — "and clear it for the use of the Vemathi. You are advised of this so that you may make ready for this change, if it be your will to have pity upon us. If your hearts are hardened and this plan does not find favor with you, the Lord asks only that you send a delegation to the City in order to negotiate with him."

A wave of murmurs swept the people. Eikoheh stepped

forward. "Of old it was well known, even in the City, that only the spirit-gifted among us leave the forest. Tell your Lord that if he would treat with us, he must come hither."

The messenger bowed slightly from the saddle. "Nay, Lady, that will not answer, for the Lord of the City wishes your people to see our plight before you turn your backs upon us. If you refuse to send a delegation, we can only assume that it is a matter of little moment to you, and as the matter presses us sorely, we will begin to clear the land. We will wait a month for your delegation to arrive before we begin our labors."

The answering murmurs grew angrier. "We must have more than a month," Eikoheh said firmly. "Our people are spread widely through our lands."

The messenger shook his head. "A month and one month only, woman of the forest. I can give you no other word."

Eikoheh raised both hands to still the protests from her people. "I know you are only a messenger," she said, her old voice steady, "and have no power on your own to say yes or no, but we must speak to your Lord through you. Tell him this for us, for the Orathi: we will come. It may take us longer than a month to arrive, but we will come. If you bring your laborers to clear the land, there will be trouble, for we will not leave our land. We are a peaceful people; we do not bear arms against other people, but we will force you to kill us before we relinquish to you that which is our care and charge. The forest was given to us by the gods, and even the deepest need of your people or your Lord is not sufficient to take it away."

"Ah, but Lady," he protested, "we will not take all the forest from you — only this little piece, for although it is true that the gods gave you the forest, surely you must admit the Vemathi grow while the Orathi decline. In our travels, you are the first people we have seen. Surely you no longer need all this land, having failed to prosper. We, having prospered with the gods' aid, require it of you now. It is clearly the gods' will that you acquiesce in this."

"Come now," Eikoheh remarked, her voice nettling with sarcasm. "I am willing to believe that the Lord of the City put his words in your mouth — but the gods?"

There was a low ripple of laughter. The messenger flushed. "Have a care, woman! I have Khedathi guards to teach you manners."

Eikoheh nodded. "The Vemathi have always been quick to cower behind the weapons of the Khedathi."

The man made an angry gesture and one of the blond riders moved forward, sword raised.

Without considering consequences, Zan sprang to Eikoheh's defense, interposing herself between the old woman and the rider. She flung her hair out of her face, put her hands on her hips, and drew herself up. "How dare you!" she cried at the startled young Khedatheh. "She is an old woman, thrice your age and half your height. She bears no weapon. If you want to hurt someone, get off your horse and come at me. I also bear no weapon, but at least I am nearer your size."

There was a shocked silence. The Khedatheh rider backed

her mount a pace. "I would have used only the flat," she told Zan.

"That you would consider striking her at all horrifies me," Zan retorted. She turned to the messenger. "Whether or not your Lord heeds you, tell him that the Orathi will come, even if it takes longer than a month. We are not asking you to promise the impossible — just tell him. If he has any honor, he will wait."

The messenger's voice was perfectly controlled again. "I will do as you ask, but I doubt it will make any difference to my Lord. You have heard his terms; it would be unlike him to change them." He bowed to them all. "I bid you farewell." Then he signaled to the others and they turned their mounts and cantered away. The Orathi watched until they were out of sight, then, silently, they moved away from Zan, Eikoheh, and Iobeh. One or two of them looked back, but no one spoke.

Eikoheh waited until they were out of earshot before she turned to Zan. "I wish you had not done that."

"I was supposed to stand there and watch that woman hurt you?"

"I am not that fragile, 'Tsan," she said testily. "She would have used only the flat, as she told you. The Khedathi have honor."

"I didn't know that, but even so, Eikoheh, it would have hurt you. Now they are gone, and you are unhurt. How have I done wrong?"

"You have championed the Orathi," the old woman said.

"The others will expect you to do so again."

"I don't understand," Zan said. "This is wrong?"

Eikoheh sighed. "You are a stranger. You do not understand what is at stake."

Zan spread her hands in exasperation. "Then teach me. I am not unwilling to learn."

Iobeh tapped her arm. *You will have to learn now, 'Tsan. That is why Eikoheh sighs.* She shivered. *Let's go home.*

"Yes," Eikoheh agreed. "Help me pack my things."

Just then Fafimed came over and drew Eikoheh apart. They spoke briefly while Zan and Iobeh finished packing. After he left, Eikoheh came back to them, but she seemed preoccupied. No one spoke on the way home.

FOUR

When Eikoheh, Zan, and Iobeh returned to the cottage, Karivet was there, calmly stirring a pot of *kemess*. His calm disappeared when he saw their faces.

"What is it? What has happened?"

Eikoheh shooed them onto the cushions. "We had messengers from the City. They were polite, but nonetheless it was clear that the Vemathi intend to take all the land east of the Tianneh."

"They *can't*," he said, sounding very young.

The old woman shrugged. "I told them we would not give them the forest willingly. They offered us the chance to parley with them, if we send people to the City. We have a month before they begin cutting trees."

"Would someone please explain to me," Zan put in, "why these Vemathi think they can order everyone about? It seems to me they've taken a very . . ." She hesitated, searching for a word. ". . . a very lordly tone with the Orathi, and no one seems to think it unusual. What makes them think they can just say the word and you will move away from your homes and give them the land?"

Eikoheh sighed. " 'Tsan, it is more tangled than it seems. Once there was friendship growing between our people and the City. The Vemathi are first of all traders, and they thought to trade their goods with us, and, I think, to make us like them. It worked — a little. Some of us left the old ways, built villages like this. But we learned something else: we need the forest. Even those of us who left the old ways need the forest. We discovered we could not become what the Vemathi wanted, we cannot live the way they would have us do. So they lost interest; the roads that they made were allowed to grow over, and we were left to ourselves. Our experience with the Vemathi taught us a lesson: we learned we were made the way we are because the wise gods wanted us this way. It would not suit the Weaver for us to change our color on the Loom. But the Vemathi learned a different lesson: they see our gentleness, our respect for life, and our care for the forest as weakness. They push, we give back; it is our way even as it is theirs. And then, with the help of the Khedathi — who make even the Vemathi seem gentle by comparison — they think themselves unopposable."

"Who are the Khedathi, then?" Zan asked, struggling to make sense. "People of the sword" was what the word meant.

"The blond ones," Eikoheh said, "the ones with weapons were Khedathi. They are dwellers in the desert, the dry lands," she explained, forestalling Zan's question. "The Khedathi are a fierce people, for the desert does not encourage

40

gentleness. They are much concerned with honor and skill with weapons; they believe the two are related. Over the years, some of them have bound themselves to Vemathi overlords. The Khedathi provide the force behind Vemathi highhandedness."

In the considering silence, Karivet spoke anxiously. "Has a gathering of Elders been called?"

"I'm just going," she told him. "While I'm gone, explain to 'Tsan about the *tuvahendi*. And eat some of the *kemess!*"

"The what?" Zan said as the door closed behind Eikoheh.

"It's a legend," he told her. "The *tuvahendi* are people without homes, people who spend their lives moving from place to place. It makes a good story, for we Orathi seldom travel even within the forest, and the only ones who ever venture beyond the forest's edge are the spirit-gifted. Many strange things are said of the Wanderers beside a winter's fire. It is said they are gods in disguise, come to oversee and aid their people; it is said they are shapeshifters and can take the form of beasts; it is said they are great workers of enchantments. Many things are told of them, and much is surely nonsense, but in most of the stories the Wanderers become champions for our people, sometimes at the cost of their own lives. You see, the Orathi do not take up arms against other people, so in ages past we have had need of help from outsiders."

Zan shivered. "Do the Wanderers usually come from impossibly far lands and not speak the Senathii?" Her voice was edged with sarcasm as she struggled to control her fear.

"That part is never spoken of in the tales," Karivet replied, showing no reaction to her tone. "The Wanderers simply appear mysteriously — but to people who never venture beyond their own hunting runs, any appearance is mysterious."

Zan was silent for a long moment, trying to still the quivering apprehension in her stomach. "I don't understand," she said at last. "If you all think me a — a hero out of a legend, why does Eikoheh object to my acting my part?"

Karivet sighed. "I do not think Eikoheh believes you have stepped out of a legend, but she is afraid others will see you in that light. She wants you to understand what people will expect of you, and she wants you to be able to refuse the role that people may try to thrust upon you."

"Does she want me to refuse?"

"I think so."

Zan frowned. "But why? Surely it is to your advantage to have an advocate?"

"It is dangerous for you." As he fell silent, Iobeh touched his hand and signed to him. He nodded. "Iobeh suggests I tell you the story of Emiarreh. She came to the Orathi generations ago. At that time the many clans of the Khedathi had ceased their quarreling and banded together under one powerful leader. His name was Khevvad, and he believed it was his destiny to conquer the known world. He and his troops began with the forest, cutting trees and slaughtering our people. The Orathi are not warlike; we consider life sacred. We kill only what we must to survive — and never other people, even in self-defense, since we believe that all peoples are precious to the wise gods. The Khedathi have different laws. They value honor, and their honor is somehow linked to their prowess with weapons.

"In this bloody time, Emiarreh appeared. No one knew from whence she came. She was neither Khedatheh nor Oratheh; she had neither woodcraft nor weapons skill, but she wove songs and tales that transported listeners away from their cares and troubles. At first she used her talents merely to comfort the Orathi, but as time passed and the slaughter continued, she determined to act directly against the Khedathi. She had heard that the leader of the Khedathi fancied himself clever, so she issued a challenge to him: a riddle game, in which the winner would be the one to determine the fate of the Orathi. The leader accepted Emiarreh's challenge, over the protests of many of the other clan chiefs, and the game commenced.

"For four days and four nights they riddled, and seemed evenly matched. But toward dawn of the fifth day, it began to seem that Emiarreh would prevail. That fear struck so deeply into the soul of one clan chief, named Gemerral, that he was moved beyond honor. He put poison in the cup from which Emiarreh drank. She died before she could answer one of Khevvad's riddles, and Gemerral claimed she had been struck down by the gods for meddling in the fate of their chosen people. But Khevvad suspected the truth, and to test Gemerral, he took up Emiarreh's cup to offer a toast to victory. Gemerral was forced to confess his treachery and was cast out by his people. In shame, Khevvad disbanded his army and took his people back to the desert. The Orathi were spared, and Emiarreh's memory is revered to this day."

Karivet fell silent, his eyes on Zan's face.

Zan stirred her now-cold *kemess*. The story troubled her. Emiarreh's death seemed so pointless — she was a victim of fear and spite, not one who had had the heroic death Zan had imagined when Karivet was describing the Wanderers. Finally she set her spoon down and met Karivet's gaze. "You said I was sent by the gods. Is this what you meant — sent to be a Wanderer?"

He nodded.

She bit her lip and looked back at her plate. "I can't be!" she burst out. "How can I champion the Orathi? I'm nothing special. I haven't any gifts or talents. If you're right, Karivet, and I've been sent by the gods, they've made a bad mistake."

Iobeh touched her comfortingly. *The gods are inexplicable, but not foolish. If they sent you, there are reasons.*

Zan reacted with horror. "Not you, too!" she blurted. "At least Eikoheh shows sense enough to doubt this foolishness." But even as she spoke, she wondered whether it was true. It would be like the weaver to want Zan to accept her fate with open eyes, instead of just falling into it.

Zan tried to retreat into the conviction that this was all a dream, but she found that refuge closed. It all made sense; it rang true in a deep, chilling way. She met Iobeh's anxious eyes, then Karivet's. Moved by a fierce desire for certainty, for confirmation of what she feared, she reached over and gripped the boy's wrist. "Why am I here?" she whispered.

"The Weaver strung your color on the Loom because without you, the Orathi will perish."

"Will I succeed in saving them?"

"The Weaver strings the Loom, but you choose your pattern."

She released him and he pulled his arm away. The silence stretched between them. Finally she looked away.

"Will you do it?" Karivet asked at last.

"Have I any choice?" she responded bitterly.

"Of course you have a choice," he replied, shocked.

She looked up at that, for the first time the hint of a smile softening her expression. "Not if I'm going to be able to live with my conscience. I guess your gods knew what they were doing after all. Tell me," she added, trying to ease the tension, "what will happen at this meeting of the Elders?"

"They will talk. Everyone will agree that it is terrible and no one will know what they ought to do. Eikoheh will make suggestions and Fafimed will dismiss them. Gurass will counsel caution and Shiheva will wring her hands. After an age, either Thenat or Kassi will remember us and ask to see us, or they will all agree to meet again tomorrow. Then they will go home."

Zan found herself smiling at the look of disgust on his face. "But how can there be that much to discuss? The Orathi must send someone to the City — I should think it would only be a question of whom."

"It's a harder question than you think. After all, it must be one of the spirit-gifted, and the spirit-gifted are rare. Besides us, the nearest is Ohmiden. He lives deep in the forest; it would take two weeks to reach him, and even then, he might refuse. It is said he is unpredictable."

"Why must it be one of the spirit-gifted?" she asked.

"Surely this is important enough to cause even the most deeply rooted of you to consider traveling?"

"One of the things we learned from our association with the Vemathi," Karivet said slowly, "is that we need the forest. When a few Orathi tried to move from the forest to the City, they grew ill and died. Only the spirit-gifted are strong enough to survive the separation."

Iobeh touched her arm. *It is not the will of the wise gods that the Orathi be travelers. The forest is our place, where we belong. We are its guardians, and in return it breathes life into us. We exist for the forest as much as it for us.* Suddenly she caught her brother's eye. *Eikoheh.*

Karivet shook his head. "It is true that Dreamweaving is a spirit-gift, but it is not like the others. She has given her spirit to the Loom, and it would be her death to part from it."

"Well," Zan said quietly, "if the Elders wish it, I will go to represent your people." She smiled a little wryly. "Though I will need a guide to the edge of the forest."

Iobeh gripped her arm. *You will not go alone!* she signed emphatically. Just then, as if in answer to Iobeh, Eikoheh stormed in, slamming the door behind her.

"I cannot believe I have wasted the better part of an hour in the company of such spineless idiots! They whined, they wailed, they wrung their hands — did everything except apply their minds to the situation."

But they always do that, Iobeh signed. *Why does it cause such anger today?*

"I could *strangle* that Fafimed. After all this weeping and wailing, what does he do but say that the stranger can go to the City for us! And they leapt at the idea. I was never so ashamed!"

"I have reached that decision myself," Zan said with more outward calm than she felt. "You need not distress yourself on my account."

"Don't say that! You must refuse. It is not your responsibility."

"Oh, but it is, Eikoheh. Everything points in that direction. I will go: I must."

"Ah, 'Tsan, think of it!" the old woman protested. "You would be even more a stranger there — and alone."

Iobeh slammed her fist into her open palm. *Not alone. We will go, too.*

"You *can't!*" Eikoheh cried. "You are only children."

Iobeh signed something Zan could not follow; she looked at Karivet and he translated. "We are the spirit-gifted. We have never been children."

"What other choice do you have if you want to have someone there before the month is up?" Zan asked gently. "Eikoheh, you are honorable — you would not put others into a danger you cannot bear yourself. And you think we do not understand what we are offering, but we do. Besides, there really is no other answer. If the Vemathi are anything like my people, it is easier to stop something before it begins than to interrupt it."

Eikoheh met their gazes, each in turn, searching for something. Her eyes were touched with sadness, then with resignation. "If you are determined, there is nothing else I can do. They will use you — and it is use, even with your consent, for you *don't* understand the cost. Didn't Karivet tell you about the Wanderers?"

"He did." Then, trying to set the old woman at ease, Zan added, "Maybe some winter it will be my tale told at the hearth. I am willing for it to be so."

"Such tales are more comfortable in the telling than in the living," Eikoheh pointed out. "But don't bother to argue with me. I can see that you have all made up your minds. I will speak to the Elders tomorrow. I will see to it that you have a guide as far as the edge of the forest — even if Fafimed has to go himself!"

FIVE

 In the end they were spared Fafimed's
company, since the Elder Thenat volun-
teered to be their guide. Fairly early in
their first day of travel, they crossed what seemed to be an
old, rather overgrown road. When Zan asked Thenat about
it, he told her it was left over from the time when the Vemathi traded with the Orathi, but he refused to use it as a path,
saying that it was haunted by the wise gods' anger. She tried
to get him to elaborate, but he would only shake his head
nervously.

As Thenat led them through the dense forest, Zan often
found herself marveling at his woodcraft. He never seemed
unsure of their path in the vast wilderness, he moved with
less noise than a woodland creature, and he was a fine hunter
and good cook, providing varied and interesting meals for
them each evening. He spoke seldom, and for all his being
one of the Elders, seemed a little in awe of them.

Their journey from the Tianneh River took three days. On

the morning of the fourth, Thenat pointed them in the proper direction and started away. Zan called him back.

"Why is it," she began uncertainly, "that the Vemathi need so much land? Or didn't we come by the most direct route?" she added, thinking of the overgrown road.

"We came the fastest way I know," the Elder told her. "As to why, who can answer for the dwellers in the City? They are strange — mad, perhaps — but they are used to having things as they order them. I wish you luck with them, Stranger." Then he turned purposefully and padded into the shadowed undergrowth.

After a short time the forest thinned to copses and meadowland. A little to their left, they could see the brown track of a road. They made for it. The road climbed gently, the dust scuffing slightly under their feet as they walked. Despite the heat, Zan enjoyed the sun on her face, but she noticed that Iobeh and Karivet looked around nervously. They hadn't been walking long before Iobeh turned and pointed back the way they had come. They saw riders: a Vemathen and three Khedathi, coming up behind them. They moved to the grass verge and waited for the riders to pass, but when they drew abreast, they halted.

"May the gods smile upon you," the Vemathen hailed them. "It is seldom we see foreigners in our lands. May I make bold to offer you the greetings of the City?" He accompanied his words with a polite bow which gave Zan a chance to study him covertly. He was older than the messengers who had come to the Orathi. Gray had faded his dark hair and his fair skin seemed stretched too tightly over his beaky features.

"Thank you," Zan replied, ignoring the uneasiness in her stomach. "We have been sent by the Orathi to parley with your Lord."

There was a silence; Zan looked down as Iobeh took her hand.

"What fool's errand is this? Even the odd one is little more than a child."

Zan's head jerked up as she sought the speaker, but no one's lips were moving. Her stomach fluttered and she tightened her hand on Iobeh's. "My companions are spirit-gifted," she said, "and are honored among their people."

"Permit me to be the first to bid you welcome," the Vemathen replied easily. "I am Efiran, of the House of Moirre. I trust you will accept our escort into the City. I am certain my Lord looks forward to meeting with you."

Zan nodded with what she hoped was graciousness. The man gestured to two of his Khedathi retainers, who dismounted and led their horses forward. They were magnificent beasts, black and tall, caparisoned in silver, but Iobeh backed away from them, shaking her head. *No*, she signed. *I can't.* Karivet stepped forward and stroked the nose of the nearest horse. *It won't hurt you, Iobeh*, he signed. *I can't*, she repeated.

Zan, feeling the intensity of Iobeh's reaction, intervened. "It is very kind of you to offer us —" She gestured to the horses as she realized she had forgotten the word. "But we would prefer to walk. If it suits you, you may leave one of your people to guide us and go ahead."

Efiran dismounted. "If you will walk, I will walk with you." He gave his reins to one of his entourage and moved toward them. Belatedly, Zan remembered her manners.

"I am called 'Tsan, and these are Iobeh and Karivet."

The Vemathen bowed politely. "Have you had a long journey from your dwelling place?" he asked them.

"Not long," Karivet answered. "We live on the Tianneh River; we have been traveling a mere three days. This is the fourth."

Zan noted the faint sarcasm in his tone and wondered what Efiran made of it — if indeed he heard it. As they walked, Efiran continued to try to draw Iobeh and Karivet out, and Karivet fielded his questioning with an offhand skill that surprised Zan. He managed to be perfectly civil and utterly unhelpful at the same time. She found herself wishing she had been able to deal as well with all the people who had tried to pump her about her father — she knew she had almost always ended up sounding sullen.

Efiran was not impervious to hints — even subtle ones — and after a while he fell silent. Zan had a few uneasy moments wondering whether he would start in on her, but apparently he decided against it.

After what seemed an interminable time, the road reached the crest of the gentle hill it had been climbing, and they had their first glimpse of the City. Zan's breath caught. The City was beautiful. It rose out of neatly cultivated fields, and seemed to be carved entirely of rose and white stone. Impossible and delicate, it perched on the rim of a cobalt-colored bay, with fragile towers and spires rearing up from its center. Beyond the City, the bay was dotted with islands, bits of floating green guarded by white cliffs.

Zan came out of her reverie to find Efiran's amused eyes on her. Her mouth quirked slightly. "Very lovely," she told him gravely.

"There are no trees," Karivet said. "It must get hot in your City."

"We have trees," Efiran told him. "I will show you my garden. You cannot see them from this distance."

In a short while they were within the City. To Zan, the City felt less strange than the rough Orathi village carved out of the wilderness had at first, but she could see by the way the twins' eyes widened that it was peculiar and unnerving to them. Despite her familiarity with streets and shops and houses, Zan found that the City kept its unearthliness. The wide white and rose streets were uncluttered; the light traffic — an occasional ox cart, some horses, and a few pedestrians — moved smoothly. Zan saw no street vendors or bustling open-air marketplace. Everything was orderly. After a time it began to make Zan nervous; it was too perfect. Perhaps Efiran was leading them through only the best part of town, but it made her wonder where the real people lived, the people who built the lovely stone houses, who cut the slates for the roofs, who tended the beautiful parks and gardens they passed. If the City were no more crowded than this, she could not begin to imagine why the Vemathi thought they needed such a vast tract of Orathi land, or what they really intended to do with it. The thought of a fairy-tale city like this stretching for nearly four days' travel filled her with horror.

Quite suddenly she was jolted out of her musings. Efiran had led them down a side street, and now took them up a flight of steps to the door of a fine house. "I have decided," he told them, "to ask you to rest and refresh yourselves at my home while I send a messenger to the Lord of the City. You will find it as comfortable, I am sure, as the Lord's house — and it is closer. Moreover, it is likely the Lord will not be able to see you today, as it is already past noon."

Zan felt a little uneasy and looked at Iobeh questioningly. Iobeh signed, *He is pleased with himself; he is being clever. I do not think he means us harm.*

"Thank you," Karivet replied. "It is kind of you."

"Not at all. It will make Hobann sick with envy."

"*What?*" Zan said sharply. Seeing all of their startled expressions, she felt queasy.

"I did not speak, Lady," Efiran told her, "but I was just going to say that it is my pleasure and honor to welcome you."

Without giving herself a chance to reconsider, she met his eyes squarely. "Who's Hobann?"

Efiran's face went completely expressionless. "Ye gods." Zan heard the words, though his lips didn't even twitch. She gritted her teeth together on the impossible and waited. He recovered very quickly.

"Hobann is the head of a rival merchant house. He and I both collect curiosities; it is a friendly competition of many

54

years' standing. But please, you must be weary. I must not keep you waiting on my steps while I bore you with my ancient history." He led them inside as his Khedathi entourage took the horses around to the stable.

Inside, Zan caught her breath, and she could tell by the stubborn set of Karivet's chin that he was determined not to gape like a yokel. Efiran's house was, like the City itself, elegant and imposing. Liveried servants, soft-footed and purposeful, went about their business. The entrance, vast as a courtyard, was filled with light from the glass roof. The walls were hung with lavish tapestries between brass sconces holding thick white candles. The broad, graceful sweep of the stairway led to a balcony that ran around the hall on three sides. Beyond the alabaster balustrade Zan could see doors that led deeper into the house. The floor of the entrance court was black and white marble set in an elaborate spiral pattern. In the exact center of the court was a larger-than-life-sized bronze statue of a dignified man with the clean-edged features Zan had begun to associate with the Vemathi. Spurred on by the fierce, almost desperate determination stiffening Karivet's spine, Zan gestured toward the statue.

"The founder of your family's fortune, doubtless?" she inquired blandly.

"Indeed," Efiran agreed, a wry expression on his lips. "My great-grandfather. I like to think of him watching over his descendants. But now, permit me to present my wife, Pifadeh." She descended the broad stairway as he gestured, her entrance meticulously timed.

It was clear from the moment she appeared on the scene that Pifadeh was a consummate master of her game. Despite her delicate, fragile appearance and sweet voice, she took them in hand as firmly as any drill sergeant. As soon as the introductions and small talk were concluded, she led them off through a maze of corridors to a suite of richly furnished guest rooms. Then, murmuring that she would send someone to attend them, she went out, closing the door softly behind her.

Zan looked around at the brocaded walls and the velvet-upholstered divans. Suddenly she felt she had been trapped in one of the period sitting rooms in a museum. She laughed, a little hysterically. The others watched her anxiously, until Iobeh signed — gesturing toward the furniture — *Do we sit on it, sleep on it, or just admire it?*

The plaintive look in her eyes sobered Zan abruptly. If this was strange to her, how much worse was it for the twins? She took them on a quick foray through the suite, discovering three bedrooms, each with its own massive fourposter bed, and a small (by comparison) tiled room with a garderobe, a sunken tub (though without running water), and a washbasin built into a wide shelf running along one wall. There was a graceful stoneware pitcher and a pot of soft, herb-scented soap beside the basin, and heavy cotton cloths in varying sizes hung on racks on the door.

When they had finished exploring their quarters, they all felt a little better and went back to the sitting room. Iobeh discovered that the tall windows looked out over an invitingly lush garden, and she leaned on the wide sill while Zan went to an ottoman and sat down. The distractions of their surroundings wore off abruptly, and Zan found her thoughts sweeping uncomfortably back to the strange things she had heard without hearing. She rested her elbows on her knees and covered her face with both hands. It was too much. It was all too much.

Karivet touched her shoulder gently. "It is clear you are troubled, 'Tsan," he began. "Does it have to do with this Hobann you mentioned? How did you come to hear of him?"

"That's just it," she said, her words muddied by her hands. "I was hearing . . . Efiran's *thoughts!*"

But why does that frighten her? It is like what I do.

Zan raised her head and looked at Iobeh, surprised. The girl had come away from the window and was standing beside her brother. "You hear thoughts, Iobeh?" Then Zan realized she had not been watching Iobeh's hands. She reached out desperately for her friends. "What's going on? Karivet, what's happening to me?"

Karivet's eyes went distant and his voice was flat. "You are growing into your spirit-gifts."

"Sweet Jesus," she whispered fervently. The English words sounded very strange in her ears. "But we don't have spirit-gifts where I come from," she protested.

You have them now, Iobeh thought.

Zan turned toward her, forcing a smile. "I guess so. But Iobeh, how is it that you can hear thoughts?"

Not thoughts, she signed. *Feelings: the speech of the heart.*

"I knew you could make the speech of your heart heard,

57

but I guess I didn't realize it went both ways." Something else that had puzzled Zan surfaced suddenly. "Why were you afraid of the horses? I thought you liked animals."

Iobeh shuddered; her hands moved very swiftly. *They were obedient and tame, but inside they hated — very much. They wanted to be free, and they raged at the people who forced them not to be. Couldn't you feel it? It was horrible; I couldn't bear it.*

Karivet and Zan exchanged looks, but before they could respond, the door opened. They scrambled to their feet as a young woman entered, carrying a large can of steaming, scented water. Her eyes were a peculiar, almost colorless gray, like water over stones, and her straight shoulder-length hair was a wan brown; she wore a shapeless garment of a drab color between green and gray with the badge of the House of Moirre worked in black at the shoulder. It seemed as though she were trying to make herself inconspicuous, nondescript. It nearly worked, except for the powerful presence she brought with her into the room. Her entrance riveted Zan's attention. As though sensing the interest, the woman hesitated, then met Zan's gaze with studied blankness. When she spoke, her words were oddly sibilant.

"I will fill the bath if my ladies and lord would care to bathe?"

"Thank you," Zan responded. "Baths would be welcome."

Without another word, the woman went about her task. It took her several trips, but eventually she emerged with a cloth draped over one arm. As she looked at them questioningly, Zan realized this woman expected to attend them in the bath. Zan's eyebrows rose.

"It is not our custom to be waited upon in the bath."

The woman held out the cloth to Zan, who took it. "I will lay out clean clothes for you. When you have finished your bath, ring" — she indicated an embroidered bellpull — "and I will bring fresh water." Then she went out.

The warm water felt delicious, and it took all of Zan's iron resolve to keep her from lazing about in the tub. She managed to get herself clean — even her hair — in reasonably short order, then wrapped herself in an ample towel-like cloth and slipped into her bedroom, calling to the others that she was finished. She found a garment like a caftan laid out for her, which she put on before toweling her hair dry and raking it thoroughly with the tortoiseshell comb she found on the dressing table. When she had finished, she went back into the sitting room, where she found Karivet by himself, gazing out the windows. He looked forlorn and very young.

"Where's the servant?" Zan asked quietly.

"She went away again. I'll summon her when Iobeh is done. Why? Do you need her?"

Zan shook her head. "I just wanted to be sure we were alone before I told you how special I think you are — both of you. I know this is all strange to you, but you don't let your uneasiness show. I don't know how you take everything so calmly, but I'm impressed. And I think Eikoheh would be proud of you."

His pinched expression eased into a little smile. "You're fairly good at this yourself," he remarked. "I don't know how you knew that metal man downstairs was an ancestor. I almost asked Efiran whether we had to worship at his shrine."

Just then Iobeh poked her damp head in to let them know she was finished. Karivet reached for the bellpull, but before he touched it there was a tap and the servant returned with another can of water for Karivet's bath. Zan found herself wondering whether the servants had spyholes to keep tabs on things, or whether this one was just good at her job. When she had finished filling the tub, she paused in front of Karivet and Zan.

"If there is anything else my ladies and lord require, you need only summon me." It was clearly a set phrase, and said with such lack of inflection it was almost a slap. Zan looked at the woman intently.

"Thank you," she said. "I haven't felt this clean in days. Hot water is a wonderful thing."

The woman turned away. "Not if you have to carry it."

Zan smiled at that tart comment. It was the first spontaneous thing the servant had said. "I see your point," she agreed, "and even more, I appreciate your effort."

At the first word, the woman froze. Without turning around, she said, "You do not look like a liar."

"*What?*" Zan exclaimed. "What do you mean, *a liar?*"

The woman wheeled, her strange eyes wide as she studied Zan's face. "It is what the Vemathi call my people: Utverassi — the untruthful ones. I am a shapeshifter." Then she went out.

Zan sat and dropped her face into her hands again. During this explanation, the woman had not opened her mouth once.

SIX

The silence stretched tautly for a long moment before Zan broke it. "When you mentioned shapeshifting, Karivet, I never thought it was anything but a story." It surprised Zan how normal her voice sounded. She looked up in time to see astonishment, then sudden understanding, flit across the boy's face.

"She is one, then," he said. "The world is full of wonders. The shapeshifters are half a legend among my people." He smiled crookedly. "A story to frighten children, for they do not have a good reputation. Occasionally shapeshifting is a spirit-gift, but it is rare. Iobeh and I used to try it, when we were small, but it wasn't given to us. How did you figure it out, 'Tsan? Did you hear her thoughts?"

Zan nodded, turning over the interchange in her mind. "She realized I was hearing her thoughts, and she told me. Karivet, why do the Vemathi call them Utverassi?" *Verass,* she knew, meant "truth"; *utverassi* meant, literally, "untruthful ones," liars.

As Karivet shook his head, her mind spun out further anxious questions. "Are the shapeshifters servants of the Vemathi, like the Khedathi? And do you suppose she can hear our thoughts, too?" The horror of that idea sunk in. "Could Efiran have sent her to *spy* on us?"

The boy looked uncomfortable. " 'Tsan, I don't know. Perhaps Iobeh can tell us. She can often tell whether or not someone is speaking the truth."

"I'll talk with her while you're having your bath," she told him, hiding her anxiety as well as she could until he had retreated into the bathroom. Then she allowed herself to think. What was *happening* to her? What was she doing in this crazy place, *reading minds*, for pity's sake, and talking with shapeshifters? It was strange and frightening. For Iobeh's sake, she tried to calm her jittering feelings, but she could seem to affect only the surface, not the anxious jumping in her stomach. Suddenly she felt Iobeh's hand touch her shoulder, bringing a welcome moment of calm. She met the girl's eyes and smiled.

'Tsan, what is it?

As Zan explained about the shapeshifter, Iobeh's eyes filled with wonder. When she finished, it was a long moment before Iobeh responded. *I don't know whether the servant was sent to find out about us. She is full of anger; it is almost suffocating, her rage, and there is contempt — though for whom I cannot tell. What we could do is summon her. You could ask her your questions, and I will try to judge her answers by her feelings.*

Something in Iobeh's manner touched a chord in Zan. "Will it be difficult for you, Iobeh? Uncomfortable?"

The girl nodded. *But it may be information we need to have,* she signed. *I am willing to do it.*

Zan squeezed her hand. "Iobeh, you're a wonder." Before she could lose her nerve, she went to the bellpull and rang. A short time later the shapeshifter came in. Her face was inscrutable as she regarded them.

Contempt, Iobeh signed. *Very strong.*

The shapeshifter's gaze flickered to Iobeh uncertainly. Zan, taking courage from the momentary chink in the shapeshifter's façade, spoke. "I apologize for summoning you away from your other duties for what may seem so trivial a reason. I want to apologize to you for my earlier rudeness. I meant to ask you — before surprise made me completely forget my manners — your name, and to introduce ourselves."

"There is no need," the servant said. "I will answer to whatever you call me, my lady."

Surprise. Wariness. Resentment, Iobeh signed.

"We are unaccustomed to being waited on," Zan continued, "and would rather you called us by our names than 'my lady' or 'my lord.' I am 'Tsan, this is Iobeh, and Karivet is the third. What is your name?"

"My kind do not give our names to your kind."

Astonishment. Anger. Affront.

"Do you mean," Zan asked carefully, "your kind as a servant, or your kind as a shapeshifter?"

"Shapeshifter," she hissed. "I am not a servant, I am a slave."

Iobeh went a little pale and pushed two fingers against the bridge of her nose. Even Zan flinched from the sudden, vicious anger that flashed across the shapeshifter's features.

Zan persevered, though she could feel the tension in the room like the heavy air before a thunderstorm. "Please forgive my ignorance. I know nothing of your people. What may we call you?"

Anger. And curiosity, perhaps.

"My lady, you may call me anything you like." The words were barbed with sarcasm.

Zan ignored the tone. "'Tsan, not 'my lady.' Must I make up a name for you? Isn't there something you'd prefer?" she persisted.

Bitterness, Iobeh signed, her face showing the strain.

The shapeshifter laughed. "Oh, indeed. There are many things I would prefer. I would prefer to be free."

"I would free you if it were in my power."

Rage! Iobeh signed, then reeled backward under the force of the shapeshifter's emotions.

"How dare you?" she spat, drawing herself up. She trembled with anger, and her pale eyes blazed. "How dare you offer me such a promise? It's not in your power and it never will be! Why are you tempting me? So your little friend can feed on my agony?" She glared at Zan silently for a moment; her breathing rasped as though she had been running. Zan's mute protest registered briefly in the shapeshifter's eyes, and amazement flickered in her expression before it was replaced by bitterness as she ground out, "You lie. You would never dare to free me. Your kind are all alike. You would be too afraid I would turn into a wolf and devour you."

When Zan glanced at Iobeh, the girl had both hands pressed to her cheeks. She shook her head; she was as white as cheese. Zan felt suddenly very alone. She turned back to the shapeshifter, meeting her eyes squarely. "I said it and I meant it. I do not believe in enslaving other people. And I do not think you would kill me. After all, why would you?"

The shapeshifter's smile curved cruelly. "Why not? The Vemathi say my people drink the blood of infants." Her upper lip pulled back in a feral snarl. "If that is so," she added in a chilling whisper, "I have hungered long."

Zan fought down a shiver of dread. "You're trying to frighten me," she said, suddenly convinced it was true. "In any case, even if what the Vemathi say is true, I'm not an infant. Besides, you were angry enough to do me harm a minute ago, and you didn't do anything of the kind then."

The shapeshifter was silent for a moment, her inscrutable eyes on Zan's face. "No. But then, I am bound." She held her arms out, displaying fine silver chains around each wrist, then touched another around her neck. She spun on her heel, starting for the door.

"Bound?" Zan exclaimed, startled. "By little strips of silver?"

The shapeshifter turned back, anger again blazing in her eyes. *"Don't mock me!"* Then the anger drained away, replaced by a frown of puzzlement. "You really *are* that naive." There was wonder in her tone, mixed with the faint sting of what Zan began to think might be habitual contempt. "The chains are spell-wrought, to keep me in this shape. I can't touch them." To demonstrate, she tried to take one of the wrist chains between two fingers. She couldn't close her fingers on it; the way her fingers were kept apart by some invisible force reminded Zan of the way like poles of a magnet pushed apart. The shapeshifter's lips twisted bitterly. "A gift from my Vemathi masters." Again she started away.

"Wait! Did they — the Vemathi — send you to spy on us?"

Spy! The shapeshifter's disgusted thought rang in Zan's mind, though when she spoke, her tone was even and rather colorless. "I wouldn't give my Vemathi masters the time of day unless they beat it out of me." Then she strode to the door and went out, slamming it behind her.

Iobeh smiled wanly at Zan. *She meant that. I don't think we need to worry about her on that score.*

"No," Zan agreed. "Are you all right? I could tell that was painful."

Yes. But I'll recover. She has very powerful emotions, and even without provocation she is full of anger. It's odd. Iobeh shook her head, bemused. *Her anger is very like the anger of the horses.*

Vividly, Zan recalled the caparisons of silver on the horses, and shivered, remembering what the shapeshifter had said about being bound in one shape. "The *horses!* My God." She saw her horror reflected in Iobeh's eyes, so she made herself shake her head. "I'm letting my imagination get the better of me," she said, forcing herself to feel the conviction she put into her tone. "Who could be so cruel?"

At that point Karivet rejoined them, dressed in a gilt-trimmed tunic over a pair of loose silk trousers. They related the exchange with the shapeshifter. He listened attentively, and when they had finished, he smiled with relief.

"It is comforting to know that we needn't worry about her ferreting out our secrets, but she sounds terrifying. Would you really free her, 'Tsan?"

Zan shrugged. "If I could, I would. Right now, though, I don't see how. We dare not do anything to offend our hosts until we have negotiated with them."

Further discussion was interrupted by a knock on the door. It was Efiran, who had come to fetch them to tea. He smiled kindly at them.

"I trust you are refreshed. Karivet, I promised to show you trees, so we will take our tea in the garden."

He led them through the stone halls, down a wide flight of stairs, and out into the lovely enclosed garden they could see from their suite. It was a lush green place, full of the quiet speech of two fountains. There were many flowers, and the trees, though nowhere near the size the twins were used to, were enough to give the place a measure of the cool mystery of the forest. Efiran settled them on stone benches near one of the fountains while servants spread the meal out before them. Pifadeh poured tea into delicate cups and passed them around. Karivet and Iobeh eyed the fragile china with a mixture of distrust and awe until Zan surreptitiously demonstrated how to hold the dainty things.

Before Pifadeh had finished pouring, they were interrupted.

"I thought I'd find you here. Am I too late for tea?"

Zan turned and saw a girl of about her own age. She looked very much like Efiran, with the same fierce nose, but she was not dressed as a daughter of the house. Instead of an embroidered caftan, she wore a plain, rather faded knee-length tunic and a pair of worn sandals. Her hair was braided and pinned severely to her head. Oddest of all, she wore a sword, slung over her shoulder in the Khedathi fashion. As soon as she noticed Zan and the twins, she backed away.

"I'm sorry, I didn't realize you had company."

"Vihena, stay," Efiran said quickly. "You must meet our guests: Karivet, Iobeh, and 'Tsan. They have come from the Orathi to speak with the Lord of the City. This is my daughter Vihena."

"I thought the Orathi didn't travel — and I've never seen hair *that* color."

Zan caught herself on the edge of responding, but realized that the words had not been spoken aloud.

"I'm pleased to meet you," Vihena said. "I hope you will enjoy our City."

"Thank you," Karivet replied.

Vihena sat down on a bench opposite them and took a cup of tea from her mother. The fragile china looked overly delicate in her hand, but her movements were deft. She studied the guests with frank curiosity while her father turned back to them.

"I have informed the Lord of your arrival, and he sends his greetings. He regrets he is unable to meet with you now, but he asks me to invite you to a banquet this evening, to be held in your honor. He also bids me to continue to make you welcome here, since building is going on at his palace and things are in disarray. I trust this will be satisfactory to you."

And if it isn't? Iobeh signed.

A pity, Karivet responded.

Zan suppressed a smile. "Thank you. We are grateful for your hospitality."

Vihena's eyes sharpened with sudden interest. "You're talking to one another, aren't you? It's like the Khedathi hand-language, isn't it? Only I don't understand it. Do all the Orathi talk like that?"

Iobeh shook her head.

"My sister is mute," Karivet said stiffly. "It is how we speak together."

Mute. Zan heard Efiran's startled thought: *Why send a mute child to a parley? There is something odd here.*

Vihena looked at Iobeh and smiled suddenly. "I thought you were just shy."

Iobeh smiled back and signed.

"She says, 'I'm shy as well,' " Karivet translated.

Vihena laughed. "I don't blame you." She turned to Zan suddenly. "And where are you from? You're not Orathi, are you?"

"I am now."

"Well, what were you before?"

"I have always been a stranger," Zan said softly. It was true, too; she had always tagged along after her father, without any real place of her own or friends her own age. With a twinge of the old loneliness — and newer grief — she remembered telling her father angrily that the closest thing she'd ever had to a home was Logan International Airport. She forced herself back to the present as Vihena asked another question.

"What's it like, always being a stranger?"

The question cut too keenly. Zan's throat began to thicken and her eyes to sting. She couldn't cry *here!* Out of a desperate need to deflect Vihena's questions, Zan struck back. "I think you know what it's like — I have seen no other Vemathi who carry swords."

Dead on the mark, and a hard hit — though I dare say I deserved it, Vihena thought.

Pifadeh eyed her daughter with a quelling look which Vihena met with a slightly sheepish smile. "I beg your pardon, 'Tsan, for my mannerless questions. My curiosity frequently gets the better of my upbringing." At this last, mother and daughter met each other's eyes, their faces showing mixtures of defiance and apology. The tension shifted subtly away from Zan.

"It's quite all right," Zan said, beginning to relax now that an end had been put to the questions. "Efiran, will there be a chance for us to speak seriously to your Lord at this banquet, or will it . . ." She paused, fishing for words.

". . . will it just be to welcome us?"

"There will be dinner and speeches, then perhaps some singing and dancing. I doubt very much that there will be any time for discussion. That sort of thing is best left to the morning hours, is it not?" Under the words, clearly, Zan heard something else. *The Lord will not meet with them any sooner than he must. We must have time to take their measure.*

"A banquet will be pleasant," Zan said mildly, "but only if we are able to meet seriously with the Lord tomorrow. I would not have his concern for our tiredness, or anything else, serve as an excuse not to begin tomorrow."

Efiran looked at her, startled. "Of course not. I am sure the festivities will not go on too late."

"Even if they do," Zan pressed, "we will consider it an affront if our meeting with your Lord is put off."

Shrewd, he thought. *Their appearances are deceptive. I must caution my Lord. They are so young — without my advice, he will underestimate them, just as I have done.* "I understand you perfectly, 'Tsan, and I admire your dedication."

Zan's head had begun to ache. She stifled a sigh, then felt Iobeh's light, reassuring touch on her arm. *Can we go indoors?* she signed. *I'm tired of these people — they're full of worry.*

Karivet spoke up. "My sister asks, since there is this banquet tonight, would it be possible for us to rest for a while? We are not used to being away from the forest, and it tires us."

72

"Of course," Pifadeh responded promptly. "Vihena, would you take them back to the guest suite?"

Vihena complied with grace. When they reached the door of the suite she hesitated, and Zan heard, as clearly as speech, her thought that she'd like to be invited in to talk to these odd people alone. But Zan, whose head felt as though it were full of hot coals, ignored her unspoken hope.

As soon as the door was shut behind her, Zan went to a divan and lay down. "My head is on fire," she moaned.

"I remember," Karivet said quietly. "Spirit-gifts do that sometimes, especially when you aren't used to them. Perhaps it will help, 'Tsan, if you try to sleep."

Obediently Zan shut her eyes, but sleep wouldn't come. Her head pounded while scraps of other people's thoughts swirled inside it. She was vaguely aware of Karivet and Iobeh's concern, but she couldn't find the strength to re-assure them. Over and over her thoughts circled anguished around the questions of what, and why, and how. Other people's thoughts buzzed in her brain like hornets. She couldn't sleep; she couldn't even begin to relax. Finally she could bear no more. She sat up suddenly, put both hands over her ears, and said aloud, in English, "I shall go mad!"

Very likely, a voice retorted sharply. *And I with you.*

But that was English, she thought. *I am losing it.*

Thoughts have no languages, or all languages, the voice explained, exasperated.

Zan was so startled that she opened her eyes. To her surprise, the shapeshifter stood looking down at her, her lips pressed tightly together.

"How did you get in here?" Zan demanded.

A faint quirk which could have been caused by amusement tugged at the shapeshifter's lips as she pointed to the door.

"Very funny. What do you want?"

How did you learn to hear thoughts? the woman replied.

"It just started, all by itself. Look, will you go away? I have a shocking headache and I'm in no mood for idle pleasantries."

There is nothing idle about my presence here; your distress summoned me. Somehow her tone wasn't soothing or comforting; she seemed reproachful. *The thought-speech frightens you. It shouldn't. Don't fight it. Relax. Try answering silently; sometimes that helps.*

How do you know so much about it? Zan thought, her pain making her grumpy. But it seemed that her headache was subsiding slightly.

It's how my people communicate with one another. I didn't know other peoples could — the Vemathi can't. Do your little friends do this too?

Iobeh hears feelings, Zan found herself answering. She hadn't meant to tell the shapeshifter that. It alarmed her. She tried to close off her mind. The pounding in her head redoubled. She shut her eyes and pressed the heel of one hand against her brow.

Don't fight it.

"But I don't *want* to hear what other people are thinking all the time!" Zan cried. "I don't want to know! No one will ever be able to have secrets from me. I don't want to be *that* different from everyone else!"

It is too late for that. The thought-speech is not a thing that can be denied. You are different. You must live with it.

Zan looked at her in horror. "You're a terrific comfort," she snapped.

I didn't come here to be comforting, the shapeshifter retorted with an edge of contempt. *One can't change one's nature, but one can learn to control the thought-speech. You can learn not to listen, if you wish to cripple yourself with scruples. Concentrate on hearing silence — that usually works at first.*

How do you hear silence? Zan demanded.

The shapeshifter's mind went suddenly still. Zan's mind was full of the sort of thick, nearly tangible silence of an empty church. Her headache eased; it was a tremendous relief. Carefully Zan took the silence to herself. The welcome stillness in her mind made her smile.

"Thank you," she said aloud, holding the silence in her thoughts.

"Don't thank me. That sort of thought-distress is contagious. Your poor little friend — Iobeh, is it? — was probably having an awful time with you so close to her. I could hear your pain and complaints even up in my quarters." Without another word, the shapeshifter went out.

Iobeh? Zan thought, but heard no answer. Experimentally, she tried wishing Iobeh, with her gentle hands and smile, were with her. After a moment the girl came to the door of the inner room. Feeling triumphant, Zan grinned at her. Iobeh smiled back.

"I'm feeling better," Zan told her. "Are you all right?"

Iobeh nodded. *Did you sleep?*

"No. I argued with the shapeshifter. It helped." She noticed then that the sky outside the windows had deepened to twilight. It was later than she had thought. "Look at how late it is getting," she added. "When do you think they'll come for us?"

Iobeh shrugged. *I'm going to change,* she signed. *I want to wear Eikoheh's weaving — it makes me think of home.*

Zan's eyes lit as she nodded. "That's a good idea," she approved. "We all should. After all, they're expecting foreigners. We might as well give them a good, outlandish show. Too bad we haven't got tanned hides like Fafimed's."

SEVEN

The banquet hall of the Lord's palace was a vast white and silver room. Empty, it would have looked like a snowscape. Now, full of people, the room swirled with dizzying color. Even the servants wore bright livery. Great brass and crystal chandeliers, dazzling with candles, hung over tables set with elegant china and silver. The head table, on a raised dais at one end of the hall, had place settings on only one side of it. As the Orathi guests were escorted to these places of honor, Zan realized with discomfort that they would be on display for the entire banquet.

The food was lavish and the company merry, but Zan, seated between Iobeh and Karivet, felt cut off from the other guests. Iobeh sat beside Efiran, who skillfully kept up a one-sided conversation with her, while at Karivet's side was a plump matron who spoke to him in the syrupy coo some childless adults use with small children. Zan was acutely aware of the many curious eyes upon her, but with Karivet and Iobeh's attention occupied, she was unable to talk with anyone. She found herself wondering whether her hosts had intended to isolate her so effectively — and if so, why. The whole situation made her feel that she carried some deadly contagion the Vemathi were trying to contain.

She hadn't liked her first impression of the Lord of the City. He was younger than she had expected, and a great deal slimier. The Vemathi were handsome people, full of dignity and grace, and their Lord was strikingly attractive. However, his slick charm and the studied quality of his politeness screamed insincerity at Zan. And she disliked the way he had lingeringly kissed her hand; it had taken all her resolve not to scrub her hand on her tunic the moment he released it. After his long and rather flowery speech of welcome, he had had them escorted to their seats, not giving them the opportunity to do more than stammer their thanks. The encounter made her remember a wine-and-cheese gathering at which her father's publisher had deftly swept them away from someone she later realized was a would-be writer. It had set her teeth on edge.

When the last of the dishes had been cleared by the ever-attentive servants, the speeches began: a lot of platitudes about how pleased everyone was that they'd come. Zan's polite smile wore thin long before she was done with it. Finally the speeches drew to a close. Zan's hope that they might be able to escape was dashed when there was a stir in the musicians' corner, and one of them came forward.

"Oh, you lucky boy," Zan heard the matron say to Karivet. "You're in for quite a treat. That's Hobann's minstrel."

Zan's interest came alive at the mention of a familiar name. Efiran had told her that Hobann collected curiosities; she sat up straighter to observe the minstrel. He was a Khedathen. He held a stringed instrument that resembled a small harp. Taking a small silver key from around his neck, he began tuning strings while the hall quieted. When it was utterly still, he put the key away and looked around at the courtiers. He gathered their attention with his dark, arresting eyes. Then he began to play. The music was strange to Zan's ears, but haunting. He played the verse through once before he added his voice, a pure, silvery tenor. The music was too intricate for Zan to follow the words, but she felt Karivet stiffen beside her. She nudged him. *What is it?* she signed under the table.

He's bold, he responded. *It's a song about the Wanderers.*

When the minstrel had finished the song, during the applause, he glanced for the first time in the direction of the Orathi delegation. His eyes met Zan's and his lips parted in surprise. He looked away quickly, but a blush tinged his golden skin. Zan wondered what had caused his obvious embarrassment before she remembered Karivet's comment: a song about the Wanderers. She nudged Karivet under the table. *I don't look like a Wanderer, do I?* she signed.

He smiled ruefully. *You do not look like an Oratheh.*

At that moment the matron, sensing Karivet's wandering attention, reasserted herself by asking another question, and he left Zan to her thoughts. Zan gnawed her lip, her mind spinning the implications idly as the minstrel began another song. Gradually the music wove her into its spell, and she found herself wishing he would never stop playing. Though his music was foreign to her, it was very lovely. At last, however, he did stop and went back to sit with the other musicians, who began tuning their instruments. As he rejoined them, she noticed that his was the only fair head in a crowd of dark ones. Her eyes narrowed; Hobann collected curiosities.

As the musicians tuned, people began to get up and stretch, milling and talking while servants moved the lower tables out. Suddenly the musicians struck up what could only be dance music, and some of the courtiers began to dance. Zan watched them as they wheeled and spun in intricate patterns, until a light touch on her elbow distracted her.

"I wonder if I might have a word with you, Lady?"

It was Hobann's minstrel. Up close she could see he was barely older than she, and for all his polished manner he seemed rather nervous.

"Certainly," she replied, then looked about for an extra chair.

He regarded Efiran and Karivet's matron doubtfully. "Perhaps you would care to dance?"

Zan's eyes went to the graceful courtiers, and she was suddenly conscious of her gangling legs and awkward arms. "God, no," she blurted, then recalled herself. "I thank you, but I have no talent for dancing. Perhaps," she added, "we could go for a walk instead? I have been sitting a long time."

"I am delighted to be of service," he responded with a small bow, then helped her to her feet. As she rose, she touched the twins' shoulders, questioning.

We'll be all right, Iobeh signed, and Zan nodded.

The minstrel guided her through the crowds. He led her through an open archway onto a garden terrace where candles set in colored glass bowls added festive color to the light from the hall. It was blessedly cool on the terrace; music and voices from the hall followed them only faintly. Zan breathed the scented air deeply. Somewhere nearby a plaintive night bird called.

"This is very pleasant," she said. "I hadn't realized how stuffy it had gotten inside."

"The speeches cause that," the minstrel said, deadpan. "All those warm compliments." Zan smiled, but he hurried on before she could speak, suddenly sounding ill at ease. "I asked to speak with you so I could apologize for the song. It was in my mind to honor you, our guests, with a song of your own people. Unfortunately, I only know one Orathi song, and it was my unspeakable luck it was *that* song. I am often impertinent, but I'm neither so shameless nor so daring as to sing a song about the Wanderers *to* a Wanderer — I simply did not know." He spread his hands. "One does not expect to meet a legend in the flesh."

Zan looked at him, unsure how to respond. Then she realized her silence was making him more uncomfortable. "You make it clear that no offense was intended," she said carefully, "and, as you said, one does not expect to meet a legend in the flesh. But the truth of the matter is, I haven't yet gotten used to thinking of myself as a legend. It would never have occurred to me to take offense at your song."

He nodded. "I supposed as much when I saw no outrage

in your face, but" — and here his expression became enigmatic — "it will have occurred to every courtier in the hall to be offended on your behalf. Now, you see, they will assume that I have groveled abjectly before you, and will spare me their censure."

Zan hid a smile. "Just like that? Do you feel your return to grace was too easy? Perhaps I should make you grovel just a little."

He raised a hand as though to fend off her words. "No, no. It is impossible to grovel just a little. Groveling must be total, or it is pointless. Shall I grovel for you? I'm rather good at it, though it is immodest of me to say so."

"I believe you, you don't need to demonstrate," she replied, laughing. "Just tell me your name. I fear I wasn't attending when you were introduced."

He hunched his shoulders, the lively spark of mischief wilting into ruefulness. "Even if you had been listening, it wouldn't have helped you. The Vemathi refer to me as Hobann's minstrel, or call me Singer to my face. The name given me at my birth is Remarr, though few people remember it. But if we are trading names, how shall I call you, Lady Wanderer?"

She made a face. "Not that, certainly. The name given me at my birth was Alexandra Scarsdale, but the Orathi call me 'Tsan, which I prefer. Now I hope you won't mind if I indulge my curiosity, Remarr. Is it unusual for a Khedathen to be a minstrel?"

"I'm not a Khedathen." As her eyebrows rose, he added, "I have no sword."

Zan heard the deep bitterness in his words, and remembered that the word *Khedathi* meant, literally, "people of the sword." "You look like the Khedathi," she said, puzzled.

"Indeed. And I was born in the desert. However, those facts alone do not suffice to make me belong there, just as my love of music and preference for the comforts of the City do not ensure my welcome here. But there," he went on, bitterness vanishing, "I mustn't cry my troubles on your cloak. To answer your question, it is not unusual for the Khedathi to sing, but it is unheard of for them to do nothing else. And the harp is not a common instrument in the desert."

Despite Remarr's light tone, Zan felt as though a door had been firmly shut on questions about minstrels and the Khedathi. She fished briefly in her mind for a good conversational gambit, but her conscience pricked her. "I'd better go back," she said with regret. "Iobeh and Karivet will be wondering what has happened to me."

"A moment, please. Rumor has it that you are staying with Efiran of Moirre. Is that true?" At her nod, Remarr's easy manner faltered and he looked a little unsure of himself, vulnerable. "May . . . may I come visit you there?"

Zan was startled but pleased. "I hope that you will."

"Oh, I shall." He smiled engagingly. "It will drive Hobann wild, but things have been dull lately." He escorted her back to the head table, then disappeared into the crowd.

Karivet's matron had lost interest and left him, and even Efiran had moved a short distance away. The twins greeted Zan gratefully, which made her feel guilty for deserting them.

"Do you want to leave?" she asked them. "I'll ask Efiran if we may."

They both nodded. Zan noticed how wan Iobeh looked. *Are crowds especially difficult?* she signed to her.

I hate this, the girl signed back.

Efiran agreed they had stayed long enough. In a short while they were settling down for the night in the comfortable bedchambers of the House of Moirre. As she lay looking up at the ceiling, Zan wondered what would happen at their meeting with the Lord the next morning. But she was tired, and soon she fell asleep.

 *The fire had sunk to sullen embers and the lamp had guttered low, but still Eikoheh sat beside the hearth, her hands deftly carding wool while her thoughts ranged far. Suddenly a thump on her door startled her. She blinked, wondering if she had imagined it, but no, it came again, and with it a voice.*

"Dreamweaver! Let me in."

She leapt up, the carding combs forgotten on the hearth. "Ohmiden?" She flung the door open and stared at the hunched old man. He wore an oversized tunic of badly cured rabbit skins; he smelled rank and his gray hair was rather greasy. But his eyes were deep, shadowed with mystery and pain — the eyes she remembered. "Ohmiden! Dear gods. Well, come in. What brings you here?"

He snorted. "Necessity. What else? I had a dream-message

that concerns you. It's about the twins. I tried to ignore it, but it wouldn't give me any peace."

"What? Tell me!"

"Aren't you going to offer me anything to eat? And perhaps a bath?"

Eikoheh rounded on him. "You can stuff yourself out of my pantry until you burst and wash yourself until there's nothing left, but for the sake of the gods, tell me first."

He laughed shortly, then gestured toward the loom with his chin. "Hasn't she taught you patience?"

Eikoheh pressed her lips together, not trusting herself to speak. Ohmiden laughed again.

"I can see that she has. Thirty years ago you'd have been at my throat by now."

"If you knew how close I am to that point, you wouldn't toy with me. Tell me!"

"I dreamed of the twins — and of a stranger, a tall woman with hair like the fire of the gods. Eikoheh, it's bad; the stranger is a friend, but they are all beset with dangers. You'd better weave them a Fate, and put in some good strong allies, for they'll need them."

Eikoheh's face blanched. "Merciless gods," she breathed, "I don't think I have the strength."

"I'll help you."

She looked at him, her eyes widening in surprise.

"It's not just the twins, Eikoheh. The fate of all the Orathi rides on this. I dreamed, and in the dream I saw the three of them, holding the forest and all our lives in their hands, and I could tell by their faces that it was too heavy for them."

85

His voice turned brisk. "Now I'm going to fix something for us to eat, and then you're going to sleep. In the morning we'll string the loom with their colors, and begin to weave a Fate for all of us."

EIGHT

The morning dawned overcast, heavy with the threat of thunder. It struck Zan as an ominous sign. The twins looked tired, especially Iobeh, whose eyes were smudged with heavy shadows. After they had risen and dressed, Vihena came in to take them to breakfast. She greeted them cheerfully and asked them how they had enjoyed the banquet.

"It was very nice," Zan lied. "Weren't you there?"

Vihena wrinkled her nose. "Gods, no. Mother doesn't trust me to behave. She says" — her voice changed to a rather good imitation of Pifadeh's precise speech — " 'If you must hold poor opinions of your peers, you must learn the discretion to hide your opinions.' I haven't learned discretion yet." Her eyes glinted mischievously. "Nor have I learned how to dance, but we won't tell Mother *that*. In any case, I'm glad you enjoyed yourselves."

She led them down to the breakfast room, an airy chamber that overlooked the garden. Pifadeh, Efiran, and a little girl were sitting at a table set for seven. The little girl was about six, Zan guessed, and she had her mother's delicate features, except that her jaw showed a trace of Efiran's square one. "That's my sister, Anfeh," Vihena whispered. "She's terribly spoiled."

Efiran rose to greet them. "I trust you spent a restful night," he said. As they murmured polite responses, he seated them at the table and Pifadeh served ham and eggs from an enameled chafing dish. Vihena took her seat with less ceremony and buttered a breakfast roll for herself.

Anfeh studied each of the newcomers in turn, staring at Zan last and longest. Her gaze had an unblinking character that seemed almost reptilian to Zan. When she had looked long enough, she said abruptly, "Your hair is a funny color. You'll have a harder time than even Vihena finding a husband."

Zan blinked at her. "I'm not looking for a husband," she replied. Out of the corner of her eye she caught Vihena's agonized blush.

"That's what Vihena always says," Anfeh said, her tone spiteful. "I don't believe her, either."

Zan was so surprised that she lost her hold on her mental silence. Thoughts from around the table buzzed in her mind. She was aware of Efiran's tolerant amusement at his youngest, of Pifadeh's resignation over her eldest's eccentricities, of Iobeh's discomfort at Vihena's embarrassment, of Karivet's distaste; but overriding all of these was Vihena's thought that she would give *anything* to be a Khedatheh and not the ugly daughter of the House of Moirre.

Zan met the challenge in Anfeh's eyes. "I was taught that it is more important to be beautiful on the inside than on the outside," she said quietly. "You might do well to think about that, Anfeh."

"I'd rather be beautiful on the outside," the little girl retorted. "It's what shows."

"The other sort of beauty shows, too — as does its lack," Karivet remarked with deceptive mildness.

Anfeh glared at him, but before she could think of an adequate retort, Pifadeh intervened.

"These are guests, Anfeh," Pifadeh told the child calmly. "And it is rude to argue at breakfast."

Anfeh's eyes widened at her mother's reproof. "But didn't you hear what they *said* to me?"

"Indeed I did," Pifadeh replied. "I think it a tribute to their own good upbringing that they did not speak far more harshly to you, for you were quite beyond the boundaries of propriety."

Anfeh's unwavering gaze dissolved into a vivid blush, and she riveted her attention on her plate. For the rest of the meal the conversation returned to the rather formal tone Zan had come to expect from Efiran and Pifadeh. Despite the comparative comfort of the expected, Zan couldn't quite maintain her mental silence and kept catching bits of random thoughts, usually Vihena's curiosity and gratitude. Apparently Vihena was unused to hearing anyone rebuke her sister even mildly.

When they had eaten, Efiran took them to the palace. The Lord of the City waited for them in a large, formal audience chamber. The room was filled with courtiers and servants; the Lord was seated in a huge chair on a raised dais, attended on either side by Khedathi guards and Vemathi clerks. It was not at all what Zan had in mind; she had envisioned a conference behind closed doors, with only a few advisers present — not this public setting. Suddenly Iobeh touched Zan's arm.

He is afraid of us and angry, she signed. *I fear he intends us harm. Can you hear his thoughts?*

There are a lot of people here, but I'll try, Zan signed back.

Without rising, the Lord greeted them and the hall quieted. Zan, listening to his thoughts as well as his words, realized that this was going to be trickier than she had anticipated. His conversation ran on two levels, and it would be hard to keep from getting mired in the jumble.

"I am so pleased the Orathi have come to parley with us," he said, though under the words his thoughts ran, *Miscalculation: never thought they would. Wish they'd stayed home. Much easier.* ". . . seldom have a chance to meet with our near neighbors . . ." *. . . heard the spirit-gifts were getting rare; never thought they'd have the effrontery to send us two children — and this oddity. Where does she fit in? Efiran says to be wary of her; she has an uncanny way of guessing what one is thinking. Gods. It will work — there are more people here than the Orathi see in a lifetime.* ". . . Orathi are known for their gentle hearts . . ." *I don't suppose that's true, but I'll throw it in.* ". . . can't fail to be moved by our sad plight." He paused, as if waiting for a reply.

Is he talking about overcrowding in the City? Zan signed. Karivet's nod was almost imperceptible.

"Your City is beautiful indeed," Zan said, "and the hospitality shown us is most appreciated. But we have seen no evidence of overcrowding in your City. To us, it seems that your City is orderly, beautiful, and comfortable. We certainly do not think of your situation as a sad plight. We are indeed grateful for this opportunity to make the acquaintance of our neighbors, but on behalf of the Orathi who sent us, we must inform you that we see no reason for the City to appropriate Orathi lands."

"Does it not wring your gentle hearts to see my people crammed together like beads in a box?" the Lord asked, turning his attention to Karivet and Iobeh.

"No," Karivet responded. "Your people are not crammed together; they are close, as beads on a string must be close, but there is order to it. It is your way and it suits your people. No matter if it seems unusual to us."

Condemn them to the dry lands. Are they heartless or stupid? Gods, give me words to explain. "But the City is like a necklace that has run out of string. There is nowhere room for more beads. And my people are not beads. They must be fed, and we no longer have enough farmland." *If you will not give us the land, we will take it. The Khedathi must be appeased.*

"But why the forest?" Zan asked. "Surely there must be other lands available to you. Could you not farm the islands?"

Farm the islands! His scorn was harsh, though his voice

carried no hint of it. "You do not understand the consequences of your hardheartedness."

As he spoke, another thought-voice intruded in Zan's mind. *We were promised* mainland *tracts — cleared forest lands. If that slippery Vemathen tries to swindle us, I'll see him flayed!* Zan thought it might be the Khedathen on the Lord's left, but his impassive face gave her no real hint.

Iobeh touched Zan's arm. *There is anger all around — the Khedathi, I think. And the Lord hates us. He is angry and also afraid. Go carefully.*

Zan nodded slightly. "Then perhaps you had better explain more fully."

What's the use? "Indeed, I shall try." *I could have them killed.* "The real problem is the farmland." *How I'd love to tear their hearts out and leave them for the vultures.* "For generations, we have rewarded the Khedathi who have served us well with lands surrounding the City to farm. Of late, farmland has grown scarce. The desert encroaches; the City expands. Notwithstanding, our faithful retainers must have their reward. This is why we need Orathi lands." *And we will have them, whether you will or no.*

"Then, if I understand you, you need Orathi lands in order to fulfill pledges your people have made to the Khedathi. In short, you have promised that which is not yours to give. Surely this is not an honorable course."

How dare she talk of honor to me! "You do not understand. You understand neither me nor the Khedathi. I, and my ancestors before me, promised the Khedathi lands that were not mine to give — I admit it! But it was necessary.

92

What the Khedathi want, they take; only their sworn word will check their desires. They take as they please unless they bind themselves with an oath. Though you do not know it, it is the strength of Vemathi promises that has kept Khedathi wolves from Orathi throats for generations. The continuing safety of your own people has been assured solely because we, the Vemathi, offer those who desire it an honorable way to escape from the desert. This is the only reason they have not overrun your lands. Now it is time for you to show your gratitude — or not. The choice — indeed, our very fate — rests with you. The Orathi may agree to leave these lands peacefully, allowing the Vemathi to keep their oath — and their hold — on the Khedathi, or you may refuse, and plunge the land into a bloodbath."

Zan shivered. There were no thoughts running contrary to this speech. The Lord meant it; it was true, or he believed it was. *He meant that,* she signed. *What should we do?*

Karivet raised his head. "It would have been better, Lord of the City, if you had told my people this at the beginning. Now we do not know what to think. You have tried to cheat us, hoping we would be unable to send anyone so that you could claim our lands for your own. What you tell us now has the ring of truth, but we have learned caution."

Ask to speak with the Khedathi leaders, Iobeh signed. *I want to know their feelings before we commit ourselves.*

"My sister asks that you permit us to speak with the leaders of the Khedathi — the people to whom you made your promises."

Shrewd little beasts — their looks are deceptive. Small won-

93

der Efiran counsels care. Spirit-gifts. The Lord turned to the Khedathen beside him. "This is Belerann, who speaks for the Khedathi who serve in the City Guard."

Ask him for the truth, Zan signed. *Ask him what would make the Khedathi reconsider conquest if we do not give them the land.*

"You have heard what the Lord of the City has said. Is it true? Would your people raise swords against my people, who bear no arms?" Karivet asked, his voice steady.

The Khedathen stepped forward. "The Vemathi promised us land if we served them faithfully. If they break their oath, the City will fall. We entered a bargain in good faith. In honor, the lands are ours, and we would take them. If your people were to resist us, they would be hurt."

"Is there nothing that would change your mind?" Karivet pressed.

"My people have been promised a land where rain falls. We have served faithfully and are worth our hire. Only a decree of the gods could change our hearts." *And these soft forest children will not dare to ask the gods.*

Oh, that fool! the Lord thought. *What made him say that? What if they know about Windsmeet? It could slow things down.*

Winds-meet, Zan improvised, signing. *Does it mean anything to you?*

A place — in the desert, Iobeh responded.

Zan gambled. "If only a decree of the gods will stay your hands, then we will journey to Windsmeet to ask them for one. Will you agree to wait for the gods' decision?"

There was a gasp in the hall. The Khedathen bowed. "The Khedathi will wait." *Their looks belie their courage — or they are foolhardy indeed.*

The Lord's thoughts were full of consternation and distrust. "I can order no one to accompany you — it is too dangerous a journey. How will we know what the gods reply?"

The Khedathen Belerann turned his dark eyes on the Lord. Zan heard his distaste clearly: *The weasel judges all as he himself would act.* "Who would dare to lie in the gods' name?"

Honor makes them so naive, the Lord thought contemptuously. *But how can we safeguard ourselves without upsetting the Khedathi?* The clarity of his thoughts dissolved into a jumble of half-formed notions. Zan followed tags of anxiety, fear, surprise, wild ideas, as they jostled one another, until suddenly, relief and jubilation overrode the chaos. *They're finished. It will never work — they haven't all the players. And the desert will kill them. We'll put a limit on the time . . .* "The Vemathi will wait a year and a day. After that, we will assume you have come to grief. It is a perilous journey to Windsmeet, as you surely know." *And if that is not certain enough,* a slimy insinuation whispered, *we can make it so. There are ways to be sure — and the desert is a wide and lawless place.*

Zan felt sick. What had she gotten herself and her friends into? But she was trapped. "A year and a day," she repeated. "That seems fair enough, if you will undertake to outfit us for the journey."

"Certainly, certainly." *They'll go; thank the gods. I'm*

safe. "Efiran will provide whatever you need. And now, if there is nothing more, may I suggest that we adjourn?"

As Zan and the others bowed to him, she caught a stray thought — Efiran's. *I hope the Lord has not miscalculated. They are remarkable; they might succeed. And who is the stranger, anyway?*

NINE

 When the three returned to their rooms in Efiran's house, they held a council of their own. Zan relayed as much as she could remember of the Lord of the City's thoughts. The twins looked grave.

"What do you suppose he meant by 'all the players'?" Karivet asked.

Zan shook her head. "I don't know. I'm afraid I've gotten us into a terrible mess. I should never have tried to match wits with them. I fear we'll all suffer for my mistakes."

You did the best you could, Iobeh soothed. *We would have been worse off without you.*

"I don't know, Iobeh." Zan sighed. "Maybe we should have told them they could have the lands. That's apt to be the outcome, judging from the Lord's thoughts. He called the desert a vast and lawless place — that sounds as though he won't stop at a little careful murder. If we just gave in and did what he wanted, at least we'd be able to go home and warn the others."

"The Lord has miscalculated at least once. The fact that we are here at all shows that the Lord's scheming is not always successful," Karivet pointed out. "And from what you said, Efiran fears this may be another mistake. We mustn't give up hope."

Before Zan could respond, there was a tap at the door and Vihena burst in, her eyes wide. "I just heard the news," she blurted. "You *can't* go to Windsmeet! It's deep in the desert, in the heart of Khedathi lands. If the desert doesn't finish you, the Wild Khedathi will — they don't tolerate interlopers. Whatever made you offer to go?"

"What would you have us do?" Zan demanded.

Give up, give in, go home. "I don't know. I guess there wasn't anything else you could do if you're determined to keep the Khedathi out of your lands. But it's such a long throw — there isn't much chance you'll survive the desert."

"Thank you for being so encouraging, Vihena," Zan retorted.

"I'm sorry. It's just that I don't want to see you come to grief."

"If we're out in the middle of the desert, you won't see it," Zan snapped.

Iobeh clutched her arm. *You've hurt her. Please don't be unkind.*

I suppose it isn't any of my business, Vihena thought sadly. *I wish they liked me; they might understand me.*

At Vihena's wistfulness, contrition washed through Zan.

"Forgive me," she said, suddenly studying her feet. "I'm angry at myself for suggesting the idea, but that's no reason to lash out at you." She looked up abruptly and met Vihena's eyes. "I've tangled this skein badly, I fear. Everyone acts as though we know what we're getting into, but we don't. I was desperate and it was all I could think of. I don't know the first thing about the desert, or the Wild Khedathi, whatever they are — or the gods, for that matter! All I know is that the Lord of the City expects us to fail and the Khedathen Belerann thinks we're fools — brave, but fools. I should never have tried to be so clever," she muttered.

Vihena looked appalled. *Dear gods. It's worse than I thought.* "You could go home," she suggested. "Just go and not come back."

Zan smiled sadly but shook her head. "Believe me, that has occurred to me, but we can't. If we give in and let the Khedathi have their lands now, it will only get worse. The forest will be eaten away until there is nothing left, unless we do *something.*" Zan turned to the twins. "I should send you home. There's no reason for you to suffer for my ill-advised attempts at negotiation."

Their expressions were mulish. *If she says we're just children, I'll shake her,* Karivet thought.

"But I don't suppose you'd go," Zan added with a rueful smile and a feeling of overwhelming relief.

And you don't want us to, Iobeh signed.

What a coil, Vihena thought. "Look, I'm going with you."

"But your father —" Zan protested.

"*My father!*" There was such a tangle of intense feeling

99

behind the words that Iobeh winced, and Zan felt a sudden surge of kinship with her. "Look at me! With my face I should have been born a boy. Then I could head the House. A girl ought to be beautiful, or at the least biddable. I'm wayward and unpredictable. I've done my best to learn the Khedathi Discipline — Khehaddi says I'm good, and she knows. But that doesn't matter here. I'm an embarrassment to my House, and the best I have to hope for is my parents' fond tolerance. Think of it: living with them for the rest of their lives, or as the maiden aunt in my sister's household. Even my father's wealth won't find me a husband — the good Houses are too selective, and my father is so proud he thinks anyone not of a major House is trying to scramble out of the gutter. There is nothing for me here; in my father's world I have no value. If you'd only let me go with you, I could do something worthwhile." She gripped Zan's arm and shook it slightly. "Please — let me go with you. Let me at least put my training to some use." Her eager face contorted painfully. "It was a cruel god who put my spirit in this City-bound body! I should have been born in the desert."

"I shouldn't let you come," Zan said, distressed. "It seems disloyal to Efiran."

"Disloyal!" Vihena snorted. "He would think you a fool for such scruples. He has his own kind of honor, but he would poison you in an instant if the Lord asked him to."

It took Zan a moment to recover from the shock; then she turned to the twins. *What do you think? Should we let her come?*

Both of them nodded.

"All right, Vihena. If you're sure you want to come with us, we'd be happy to have you."

A tremendous, relieved smile lit the girl's face. "You won't regret it. But not a whisper to my family — they would prevent it if they knew." She rose to go.

"Vihena, wait! Besides the desert, are there dangers attached to seeking for the gods at Windsmeet?"

She shrugged. "It's always perilous for mortals to confront the gods. I know of nothing more specific. I must go — I'm late for my sparring match."

"Well, thank you," Zan murmured to her retreating back. Then she turned to Karivet. "Perhaps you could tell us something." She heard his shuddering denial and suppressed a sigh. "Never mind. I'm sure we can find out somehow."

"No, wait. I'll do it. Ask me." *But please, please, let it be the right question.*

Hesitantly, listening for his change of mind, Zan took his hands and looked into his eyes. She thought for a long moment, trying to frame the right question. "Karivet, how do we seek the gods at Windsmeet?"

"At Windsmeet, a party with representatives of every kindred may call upon the gods, and one of the divine company is constrained to answer them."

Zan released his hands. "Every kindred? Like Vemathi, Orathi, Khedathi?" As the twins nodded, something the Lord had thought snapped into place. "'All the players.' Oh no."

"We need a Khedath," Karivet said grimly.

And a shapeshifter, Iobeh signed.

As if their thoughts had summoned her, the shapeshifter appeared at the door. "There is a Khedathen here to see you. He gives his name as Remarr. Will you see him?"

"Yes. Thank you."

The shapeshifter went out again without speaking. Zan watched her go, the spark of an idea brightening in her mind.

A few minutes later, Remarr was shown in. He bowed politely as Zan introduced him to the twins, but she sensed a shadow behind his cordial manner.

He's worried about us, Iobeh supplied.

With reason, I fear, Zan returned. Then she noticed that Remarr was watching their hands with interest.

So that's how they communicate with the little mute one. I should have thought of that. "I have heard a rumor that troubles me. In the City they are saying that you are going to Windsmeet. Is it so? And why?"

Karivet answered him. "Yes, it is true. The Khedathen Belerann told us it would take a decree of the gods to keep the Khedathi out of our lands. We're going to ask them for one."

"You cannot realize how dangerous it is," Remarr said urgently.

"We know that no one expects us to survive," Zan told him, managing to keep her voice level and matter-of-fact.

He looked taken aback. "And you're going anyway? 'Tsan, haven't you any sense?"

"Sense! If I had any sense, I never would have left my car on the interstate." The sudden memory was disorienting, and the English words *car* and *interstate* jarred in her ears. The bafflement she saw on the others' faces helped to jolt her mind back to the present. "What other choice is there, Remarr? Where I come from, there were — oh, generations ago — people like the Orathi, who lived in vast forests. Then my people came. They took their lands, cleared the forests, razed their villages. None of them are left. Iroquois, Seneca, Huron, Onondaga, Mohawk — all gone, the forests destroyed, the land poisoned. Perhaps if those people had had someone to send to the gods, the present would wear a different face, one less bleak for my people."

In the silence her words left, Zan heard the minstrel's thoughts clearly: *Brave hearts. I am shamed.* She dropped her gaze, suddenly ashamed of herself for hearing what he worked so hard to conceal. As she closed her mind to his thoughts, he spoke. "If you must go, then I will go with you."

"Now why would you do a senseless thing like that?" Zan asked, striving to regain the bantering tone she associated with Remarr.

He looked up with a lurking smile. "It will annoy Hobann."

The absurdity of his reasoning and the mischief in his eyes made her laugh. "That hardly seems sufficient cause," she responded.

"Well, it will. Besides, I might be of some use. I grew up

in the desert. I can guide you to Windsmeet — I even know where there is water. And if the journey is too boring, I can sing."

That was said with such drollness, it made them all laugh. *I like him,* Iobeh signed. *Tell him yes.*

Karivet spoke. "Iobeh says she likes you. So if you are really fool enough to come with us, you are welcome."

Remarr looked at Zan uncertainly. She looked back. "Will Hobann send people after you if you disappear?"

"No. He does not own me, much as he thinks he should. I go and come as I please."

"Come, then," Zan said. "We'll be glad of your company."

He nodded. "You know, I didn't come over here solely to offer meddling advice and to entangle myself in your business. It also occurred to me that you all might enjoy a tour of the City — a real tour, not just trailing about after Efiran of Moirre. What do you think?"

Iobeh leapt up. *Yes!*

"Let's!" said Karivet and Zan together.

Remarr smiled at Iobeh. "This," he said, making the sign for yes, "means yes?"

She nodded. *Yes, yes, yes!* she signed exuberantly.

"My people have a hand-speech. Perhaps I can learn yours."

Iobeh grinned. *It will give us something else to do when we are bored,* she signed. Karivet translated, matching signs to words as he spoke.

"Indeed it will," Remarr agreed. Then with a bow to

shame all courtiers, he took Iobeh's arm. "My lady, shall we go?"

So they went. Remarr proved an interesting guide, showing them parts of the City they never would have guessed existed. They spent quite some time on the waterfront, watching the little fishing boats. The twins had never seen a boat larger than the skin coracles their people used occasionally; the fishing boats were wooden, with one sail and room for about three crew members. Zan was surprised there were no larger boats, but when she asked about it, Remarr told her that wood was very scarce around the City. The boats were big enough to serve; larger boats would be wasteful.

They also went to the Street of the Artisans. There they saw a weaver whose wares were nowhere near as fine as Eikoheh's, a woodcarver who made figurines so realistic that one expected them to move, and a potter whose graceful vessels seemed to grow out of the clay on his wheel. They watched a glassblower, fascinated by his craft, but they spent the most time with a silversmith who fashioned an intricate brooch with a tiny hammer and a delicate pair of tongs. As he worked, Zan looked at his tools — tongs, chisels, hammers, others for which she had no names — and an idea occurred to her.

She leaned toward Remarr and whispered, "Would it be possible for me to get a hammer and one of those —" She pointed to the chisels, and when he thought the word, she took it out of his mind. "Chisels?"

He shrugged. "Varak? Can you spare a chisel and one of your hammers?"

The smith looked up. "I dare say. Four *kessi*?"

"Gods, man, I don't want jeweled ones, just plain for everyday. Two."

The man laughed. "Ah, Singer, I know you — you'd dicker all afternoon, keeping an honest jeweler from his trade, if I let you. Two, then."

Coins changed hands, and the jeweler wrapped the tools in a square of rough cloth. Then he went back to his work. Remarr gave the bundle to Zan, waving away her thanks. Though she heard his curiosity, he did not voice his question, for which Zan was grateful. She wasn't ready to explain her plan yet.

The afternoon passed quickly. Finally Remarr steered them in the direction of Efiran's house. As they turned onto one of the wide streets leading to the residential district, they came upon a group of Khedathi guards.

"Will you look at this?" one of them, a lean woman with a wolfish smile, asked. "At last Hobann's minstrel has found an occupation that truly suits his temperament: nursemaid."

Better nursemaid than butcher, Remarr thought, but he spread his hands and spoke meekly. "As you see, Edevvi, as you see."

What a spineless worm he is. "Well, you're not even very good at that, if you intend to let these children go off into the dry lands by themselves. Or perhaps you intend to go along?"

"Now why would I do a senseless thing like that?" he asked, with a twinkle at Zan.

"Why, indeed," the one called Edevvi retorted. *Comfort-loving coward.* "Stupid of me even to suggest it."

He shrugged. "As you say, Edevvi." He answered her sharp glance with one of such blandness that she let the comment pass, and the guards went their way with sniggers and snide looks. Remarr watched them go. *Gods, I hate them!* he thought, but when he spoke, it was with his self-deprecatory smile. "I told you I was a coward. And please, don't say anything bracing. I am used to myself, and I can't bear well-meaning pity."

Zan closed her mind, again feeling guilty for eaves-dropping. After a moment's silence, she asked, "How far is it to Windsmeet? How many days' journey?"

"On foot? A month, maybe two. Why?"

"The Lord said Efiran would provision us. I need to know how much food we should take. Should I ask for horses?"

Remarr shook his head as they turned up the little street leading to Efiran's house. "They are thirsty beasts; the water holes I can show you are too small. As for food," he said with a shrug, "we'll probably have to do some hunting. I don't think we can carry enough, even if Efiran is paying for it."

They paused at the steps of Efiran's house, and Zan clapped Remarr on the shoulder. "Just don't forget your harp. We're counting on those songs."

He gave her an unreadable look, which turned into a rueful smile when he spoke. "No fear." He started away, waving to them all. Before they even had a chance to thank him, he was gone.

TEN

 Over the next few days, Efiran was very helpful. He gathered things they would need, including a small, lightweight tent, white robes like those the Wild Khedathi wore, and a set of compact cooking utensils. The food he provided was chiefly dried stuff, nourishing but not heavy, and a great deal of it. One afternoon, when Zan was sorting through some things with him, he asked her whether she needed anything else. Zan had been hoping for such an opening.

"As a matter of fact," she began, "there *is* something. I hesitate to ask. I don't want to put you out . . ."

"No, no — I said anything, anything at all. The House of Moirre is at your service."

"Well, I've been thinking. We've grown quite used to the woman you've sent to serve us. She's a hard worker and is handy with things. We could use her. Would you be able to send her with us — if she's willing to go, of course?"

"She's a slave. What she wants has nothing to do with

anything." Zan suspected he was talking to give himself time to think; she opened her mind to his racing thoughts. *Dear gods. Could she possibly know the slave is a shapeshifter? But how could she? I can't imagine that slave* offering *any information about herself — she's as sullen as they come. And "hard worker"? Her? There's something odd here. I should refuse, but how, with the honor of my House involved?*

His thoughts gave Zan a clue about how to play out the scene. She allowed her face to show distress as she said, "Forget I asked, Efiran. You've already been more than generous. Please forgive my rudeness. I did not intend to overstep the bounds of your hospitality."

Overstep the bounds! The intensity of that thought flickered in his expression, but was quickly suppressed. *Condemn her to the dry lands! I wish I knew whether she is as naive as she appears or as cunning as my nightmares. But I cannot compromise the honor of my House.* "My dear 'Tsan. You must not imagine that the gift of a single slave could overstep the bounds of Moirre hospitality. Certainly I will give her to you, along with my heartfelt prayers that she will serve you well and faithfully." *I wish you joy of the sullen wench — and if you're up to something, I hope she knifes you.* He reached for the bellpull. A servant answered and he sent for the shapeshifter. When she came in, he said, "Slave, I have given you to 'Tsan and the Orathi. Serve them well." *This bears watching, though the damage may already be done.*

The shapeshifter turned her colorless eyes on Zan. Her mind was shut, but she looked shocked, betrayed.

Zan thanked Efiran politely, then began gathering up bundles and handing them to the shapeshifter. "We need to move these things out of Efiran's study," she explained.

It took them three trips. The shapeshifter obeyed, but there was rage in her every movement. After the last trip, Zan closed the door of the guest suite firmly behind them and waved the shapeshifter to a chair. The twins had gone with Vihena to watch the Khedathi at sword practice, so Zan knew she and the slave would be undisturbed.

"It's not what you think," she began, but the shapeshifter cut her off.

"How do you know what I think? I learned long ago how to close my mind!"

"Yes, but your face shows anger. I told you once that I would free you if it were in my power." She unwrapped the jeweler's hammer and chisel and laid them on her lap. "Hold out your wrists."

The shapeshifter was silent, her face still; only her strange eyes blazed, unreadable. Finally she hissed, "*Why?* Where's the snare? What promise are you going to exact from me first?"

"Nothing!" Zan cried. "It is true I need your help, but I will not compel you. I want you to choose freely whether to help me or not. I'm not giving you your freedom as a reward for good behavior, or on condition of a promise. If you don't want to help us, I don't want your help."

The shapeshifter studied her through narrowed, suspicious eyes. "Tell me what you need."

Zan knelt down on the floor and picked up the chisel. "Come here and give me your wrists."

"But if you free me before you tell me what you want, how can you know I will stay to hear you out?"

Zan met her eyes. "That, too, must be your choice."

The silence stretched. Finally, stiffly, the shapeshifter joined Zan and laid her arm on the floor. Zan pinned a piece of the silver chain under the chisel, then struck the chisel a sharp blow with the hammer. The chain parted and slid away from the shapeshifter's wrist. Zan repeated the procedure with the second wrist, then motioned for the shapeshifter to lie down. The neck chain was trickier, for it was not quite long enough to break easily. It took a couple of tries before it, too, slid away. Zan straightened her back, but then noticed that the shapeshifter was holding out a foot; there were chains around her ankles as well.

"They weren't taking any chances with you, were they?"

The look on the shapeshifter's face made Zan suppress a shudder. "Perhaps they had reason not to," she said, her tone dangerous.

Without giving herself a chance to reconsider, Zan struck off the last two chains. Then she went back to her chair.

Before her, the shapeshifter's outline dissolved. First she became shapeless, a sort of thick fog; then the fog coalesced into a new shape: a wolf. As it turned slowly to face Zan, she saw its strange, almost colorless gray eyes. The wolf drew its lips back from its teeth in a soundless snarl and started toward Zan. Closer and closer it came. Zan watched it, her mind a mix of wondering emotions and cold spurts of fear. She forced herself not to flinch away as the wolf reached her. It sat down on its haunches and put its head in her lap.

Tell me: what help can I give you?

Silently, forming the words with her mind, Zan explained about the journey to Windsmeet, about the need for a representative from every kindred; she expressed some of her fears of the desert and repeated some of the warnings and attitudes of others. Finally, she asked the shapeshifter whether she would go with Zan and her friends on this perilous, possibly hopeless quest.

It seemed a long time before the shapeshifter answered. *What will you do if I decline?*

We'll go anyway. Even if we cannot succeed, we must try.

The shapeshifter was silent for a moment, her wolf's features giving no clue to her feelings. *Yet with so much at stake, you have offered me a choice?* There was wonder in the thought, perhaps even respect. *I do not understand you, Stranger, but I will follow you.* She hesitated. *My name is Ychass. Do not speak it aloud.* The wolf raised its head and Ychass became a woman again. *You must not tell Efiran Moirre you have unchained me. It would be all he needs to believe you are too dangerous to be allowed to live. I trust you will not delay our departure too long.*

I hope to be able to leave tomorrow, Zan confided. *I am very tired of this City. Now I'd better go see what is keeping the twins.* She rose. Ychass watched her.

"I will stay here," she said aloud, "and await your return."

Vihena and the twins were coming up the steps as Zan started out the great front door.

"We were just coming to find you, 'Tsan," Vihena told her.

"Let's go for a walk," Zan suggested with a meaningful look in the direction of Efiran's study.

They set off down the street. Vihena led them onto quiet, wide streets in the residential district. They walked in the center of the road and kept their voices low. Zan told them that the shapeshifter had agreed to join them, and suggested that now their party was complete, they should leave. Mindful of Ychass's warning, Zan did not mention that she had unchained the shapeshifter, and an instant later she was glad of the warning, for Vihena's face creased into lines of distress. Overriding her scruples, Zan did a little conscious mental prying. Vihena was not happy to have a shapeshifter as a member of their party, even though they had explained to her about the need for a representative of each kindred; she had never liked the cold, almost haughty manner of the slave in her father's house. However, Zan knew that Vihena recognized the need and would try to get used to the idea.

Their departure was a problem Vihena could manage. She said she would tell her father she was going out with a desert patrol — she had gone before, and the excuse would give them nearly two weeks (with luck) before Efiran began to worry about her. Patrols left every other day, and one had gone yesterday. Vihena would bid her family farewell as

114

though she were going with the Khedathi, but would instead meet Zan and the others in the desert.

"There's a place called Redstone three or four hours' journey due west of the City gate. I will leave the City well before daybreak and wait for you there. If you leave two hours after noon, you should reach me by early evening. It will be hard travel, walking in the heat, but if you seem ignorant enough of desert ways to travel during the afternoon, it will help to convince the Lord that you haven't a chance of surviving and therefore aren't dangerous. But do hoard your water; there isn't any at Redstone."

"All right," Zan said softly. "We can do that for the sake of discouraging pursuit. Now I must get word to our Khedathen, so he will be able to join us as well."

"You found one? Well, I mean, you must have, if our party is complete, but who is it?"

"Remarr."

Vihena frowned, puzzled. "*Who?* Are you sure you have the name right? I've never heard of him, and I know all the guards."

"He's not a member of the guard," Zan said before she remembered the contempt of the Khedathi they'd met the other day. She cut off her explanation; time enough to worry about that when they'd escaped from the City. Fortunately, she had said enough to satisfy Vihena, and they returned to Efiran's house in silence.

At the last moment before they went in, Vihena seemed to come alive, and began chatting brightly with Karivet. It was a good thing, too, for when they opened the door, Efiran was standing in the hall. He greeted them politely, but Zan felt his watching eyes between her shoulder blades as they went upstairs to the guest suite. Once they reached their rooms, Vihena brushed away an imaginary brow full of sweat and whistled soundlessly.

"The last thing we need is for Father to begin wondering what we're up to," she remarked. "I can't shake the notion that the Lord of the City won't relax until he is *certain* you aren't coming back."

You think he might murder us? Iobeh signed. Karivet translated for Vihena.

"I fear it. But I don't think he'll try anything *here*. There would be too many questions. Speaking of questions, where is that shapeshifter, anyway?"

Ychass? Zan thought, questing.

Here. Her thought-voice was very strong. Zan looked about, startled, but saw no sign of her. *That fly — by your hand. You can tell her I'm running an errand for you.*

Would you run an errand for me? Zan asked. Sensing an affirmative, she went on. *Could you go to Hobann's and find the minstrel Remarr? We're leaving the City tomorrow afternoon; he's going with us, but he mustn't be seen leaving in our company. Tell him we plan to camp tomorrow at Redstone.*

Very well, the shapeshifter replied. The fly took to the air, and Zan looked up to find Vihena looking perplexed.

"I'm sorry — my mind was elsewhere. The shapeshifter is off on an errand for me. She should be back soon."

Vihena nodded. "You know, I'd better go. I must explain to my parents about the patrol, after all." She started for the door. Halfway there, she froze, her head coming up like that of a wild beast scenting danger. She touched a finger to her lips, then held it up in mute warning as she said with elaborate casualness, "I just realized; I'm going on patrol tomorrow, and I won't be back before you leave. I just want to wish you the best of luck."

"Thank you," Zan said. "Best of luck to you, as well. You've been a good hostess to us."

There was a faint tap on the door, then Pifadeh opened it. "I've been looking for you, Vihena. Captain Khehaddi came by earlier. She wondered whether you wanted to ride patrol tomorrow."

"Well, I was planning to. Perhaps I'd better make sure the captain knows that." She left, closing the door behind her.

I hope that won't foul things, Iobeh signed.

It's lucky Vihena's so quick, Karivet added.

I wonder how long Pifadeh was there. Zan cast her mind after the woman, but Pifadeh's thoughts were full of household matters. *I think we had a narrow escape,* she added.

It wasn't until late in the evening that Ychass returned. The first Zan knew of it was Ychass's warning in her mind: *Do not speak aloud. Tell the others. There is a spy outside your door.*

A spy? Zan demanded. *Who is it?*

One of Efiran's Khedathi. He's armed. We don't want him alerted. Warn the others.

Zan signed the message to the others, substituting *listener* for the word *spy*, which she did not know in Iobeh's hand-language. The twins' mouths shaped surprise, but even when a moth that had come in the window became the shapeshifter, they made no sound.

What happened? Did you find Remarr? Zan remembered to sign so the twins would be able to follow what was going on.

Yes. But he won't be able to travel tomorrow: he's hurt. He had an argument with Hobann — there's a noxious creature for you! — and lost. I got him as far as the garden, but I couldn't get him up here because of the watcher.

Hurt? How badly?

He will live, I think. I left him unconscious.

Some argument, Zan thought, shaking her head. *Now what do we do?*

We should leave tonight, Ychass responded. *That argument began over whether or not Remarr would commit murder — specifically, three murders — for Hobann. Hobann may know someone else who won't object.*

What about Vihena? Karivet asked.

We can still meet her at Redstone, Iobeh signed. *She doesn't expect to see us again before she goes. With any luck, they won't know we've bolted until she's long gone.*

Good thinking, Zan approved. *But how are we going to get out of here?*

The window gives on the garden, and there's a gate to the street if one knows where to look, Ychass supplied. *Do you suppose Efiran thought to provide a rope?*

There were in fact three ropes. Zan, Iobeh, and Karivet

spent a tense, hurried time sorting things and stuffing them into knapsacks. Zan made certain they packed extra desert-style clothing and water skins for Ychass and Remarr. Efiran's generosity had been unstinting and he had assumed there would be at least one pack animal, so there were satchels for each of them. Zan had a brief moment of panic when she realized there wasn't enough water in their suite to fill all the water skins, but Iobeh calmed her by reminding her of the fountains in the garden. While the three of them were thus occupied, Ychass went back to the garden to see whether she could do anything for Remarr.

They finished their silent packing, and Zan sent a mental call to Ychass, who returned to help Zan secure the ropes and lower the twins and all their gear into the garden. When all their stuff had been lowered, Zan climbed down, leaving Ychass to untie the rope so they would leave no sign that things were not as they should be.

They found Remarr where Ychass had left him, lying beside one of the fountains. They were horrified by his appearance. His face was puffy and scratched, and both of his eyes were swollen shut. Ychass had been bathing his bruises with water from the fountain, but he had not stirred. Iobeh filled the water skins while Zan and Ychass consulted. Finally it was decided that Ychass would take the shape of a mule so she could carry him and a good portion of their gear. They loaded Remarr's inert form onto Ychass as best they could.

This can't be very good for him, Zan thought.

Much better than leaving him to Hobann's care, I should think, Ychass retorted.

A pity we can't go back for his harp — we shall miss his songs.

It's there beside the fountain. When the first of Hobann's guards started in on him, his thoughts were full of hopes that it wouldn't come to harm. So I brought it. Don't you dare laugh, 'Tsan; you'll wake the house!

ELEVEN

By daybreak they had reached Redstone. They found a deeply shaded crevice in the rocks and prepared to wait. Before any of them slept, they changed into their white desert clothing. The robes were loose-fitting, with a veil that hooked into the hood, covering the nose and mouth. After they had dressed, they settled down to rest. Being smallest, Iobeh and Karivet climbed far into the crevice before they curled up to sleep, using their packs as pillows. After Zan unloaded Remarr and the gear, Ychass took her own shape and helped settle the minstrel. He moaned and stirred as Zan tried to get a little water between his bruised lips, but he did not wake.

I'm worried about him, Ychass. As the shapeshifter nodded, Zan noted the exhaustion in her drawn face. *Sleep,* she told her. *I'll watch.*

Zan propped her back against the rocks, adjusted the white hood so that it would shade her eyes, and settled down to watch. The desert had a peculiar beauty, if one took the time

121

to see it. The golden sand was wrinkled with patterns like ripples where the wind had been; the dunes stretching out before Zan's eyes looked like the marching waves of some vast, pale sea. The sky was deep blue, distant, and cloudless, and even at this early hour the horizon was shivery with heat haze. All was still: not a bird called, not a hint of breeze stirred; there were no leaves to rustle nor brooks to gurgle. There was only the sand, the sun, and the silent heat haze.

As time passed, Remarr began to stir. His moans roused Zan from her half-doze more than once. She jolted herself fully awake when she realized that Remarr had propped himself up on one elbow and was valiantly trying to get his bearings in spite of his swollen eyes.

"Welcome back to the land of the living," she said softly.

"Are you sure that's where we are?" he returned, his speech a little slurred. "I could have sworn we're in the dry lands."

His attempt at humor encouraged her and she smiled. "Would you like some water? Something to eat?"

"Water, yes. No food yet — maybe later." His elbow gave out and he lay down again. Zan lifted his head a little as she held a cup to his lips. After he drank, she let him drift back to sleep.

The next time he woke, he seemed a little better. He managed to sit up without her help, and ate some bread she soaked in water. When he had finished, he said, "How did I get here? The last I knew, I was in Hobann's stable." He looked around painfully. *"Redstone?"* he whispered, shocked. "No, I must still be dreaming."

Zan shook her head. "No, this is Redstone. I'll tell you the whole tale if you are up to it."

"I really think you had better."

She poured him another cup of water, then related the events of the night. The shapeshifter's part fascinated him and he interrupted several times with questions, but at last his curiosity was satisfied. Zan helped him change his City garb for desert robes before he again settled back to sleep. She watched him with welling relief.

She must have dozed off, for she woke with a start to the sound of footsteps. She peered out into the bright heat of near noon. A white-robed figure approached on foot. The sun glinted on the sword at the person's waist. As the figure drew nearer, Zan thought she saw a few wisps of dark hair escaping from the hood. She touched Ychass's shoulder as she pushed a gentle thought at her. *I think that's Vihena. I'm going to see. Keep an eye on me, please.*

Right, Ychass agreed, scrubbing the heels of her hands over her face.

Zan got up and left the shelter of the crevice. The figure halted and held up one hand in greeting.

"Vihena?" Zan asked.

The hand dropped. "*'Tsan!* How did you get here before me? What is going on? Why did you change our plan?"

Zan motioned to the shadowed crevice. "Come out of the sun and I'll explain."

Together they returned to the others. Ychass was sitting up, her face expressionless; Remarr was sprawled with a fold of his loose veil covering most of his face; Iobeh and Karivet were still asleep, little bundles of white behind Ychass. Vihena looked around, blinking as her eyes adjusted to the shadows. Then she sat down, cross-legged, on the sand. She did not push back her hood and veil.

"Tell me," she said quietly.

"They were going to try to kill us," Zan began. "The shapeshifter found out when she went to make arrangements with our Khedathen. He tried to stop them and got beaten senseless. The shapeshifter rescued him and came to us. We decided it would be . . . prudent to leave then instead of waiting for morning. We were counting on you to stick to the plan; I'm glad you did."

Beaten senseless? Vihena thought incredulously. *Who —Gods. It can't be.* She gestured toward Remarr with her chin. "Hobann's minstrel?"

Zan winced at the contempt in her voice. "Not any more. It was Hobann who was plotting against us. He asked Remarr to murder us. Remarr refused."

I wouldn't have thought he had it in him, Vihena thought as she studied him, unspeaking.

As if her scrutiny touched some bruise, Remarr groaned and woke. He sat up painfully, then froze when he saw her.

"You should have woken me sooner," he murmured to Zan as he raised one hand in the same greeting Vihena had used. Vihena turned her face away and did not return the gesture.

"This is Vihena, Efiran Moirre's daughter," Zan told him. "She will be journeying with us. Vihena, this is Remarr."

124

Vihena did not look at him. He shrugged ruefully, winced, then said, "I know what you would like to say: if I had any honor, I would have fought hard enough to make them kill me rather than suffer this shame. But think how inconvenient that would have been — not for me, I believe the dead are beyond inconvenience, but for 'Tsan, for your quest. 'Tsan said she needed one of every kindred. I know I'm not anything to boast of, but even so, it would have been very hard for her to replace me on such short notice. In the merciless light of day, I realize a true Khedathen would never have allowed a trifle like inconvenience to interfere with honor, but at the time it seemed like sound reasoning."

She turned cold gray eyes on him. "You make a joke of honor."

He spread his hands. "Vihena Moirre, I make a joke of everything."

Vihena turned to Zan. "I wish you had spoken to me. I could have found you ten Khedathi who would be better than *him*."

Before Zan could respond, Ychass spoke up, wry amusement in her tone. "On the contrary, I think 'Tsan was inspired. She may have gotten the only Khedathen without a sword, but she also found the only Vematheh with one. You are better matched than you'd like to admit, daughter of the House of Moirre."

"You're in no position to ridicule *me* as a misfit!" Vihena snapped. "Why don't you tell us how the Utverassi choose whom to send as tribute?"

Zan recoiled from the venom in her tone. Things had

really gotten out of hand. Before she could try to defuse the situation, Karivet's calm voice broke the silence.

"You sound like your sister," he observed.

Vihena whipped her head around to look at him; then her shoulders slumped. With a fluid gesture she unhooked her veil, pushed her hood back, and buried her face in her hands. They could all see the blush through her fingers. "I'm sorry," she said, the words muted and distorted by her covering hands. "There was no call for that." She squared her shoulders and drew a deep breath. "Forgive me, all of you," she said stiffly. "My temper betrays me into harsh words. Though I have to admit, I'm not usually brought up quite so short."

Karivet smiled at her, then answered the question that hung over the group like a thunderhead. "There's no shame in being a misfit, Vihena. No one but a misfit would go on such an insane journey. Perhaps our oddities can draw us together, not drive us apart."

The atmosphere lightened, though the shapeshifter still wore her expression of sardonic amusement. As calm returned, a niggling question wormed its way out of Zan's silence. "What did you mean, Vihena, 'tribute'?"

"Ask the shapeshifter," Vihena replied. "I shouldn't have spoken of it."

"Why not?" Ychass asked. "It was your people who thought of it, your people who imposed it." She turned to include the others in the sweep of her silvery eyes. "'And in order that we shall prevent the Khedathi from raiding your lands and destroying your nation, you shall pay to us a tribute of twenty-one slaves, shaped as we shall require, every seven years,' " she quoted in a singsong voice filled with bitterness. "I was tribute, five years ago, sent to a Vemathen who cherishes the peculiar. Usually they ask that we be sent as horses or dogs."

"Horses?" Zan asked, horrified. "You mean —"

"I have always been taught that one can recognize a shapeshifter in animal form because the eyes are human, but the tribute horses don't have human eyes," Remarr probed. "Is that true? Are they really —"

"They don't have human eyes because they have been made beasts," Ychass interrupted grimly. "Their humanity is reft from them when they are forced into beast-shape against their will. It is a cruel death, Khedathen, because their anger remains long after their reason, their essence, is gone."

Zan shuddered. Iobeh hunched her shoulders miserably while Karivet and Vihena exchanged looks and Remarr shook his head sadly.

The shapeshifter watched their reactions closely. "Aren't you going to ask me why I was chosen for the honor?" she asked at last.

Zan shook her head, sick at heart.

Ychass smiled mirthlessly. "Wise. I wouldn't have told you." Then she turned her back on the others and lay down to sleep.

Iobeh found Karivet's hand and squeezed it, her face full of pain and her thoughts in turmoil. *She frightens me; she is so full of anger.* Zan felt her fondness for the girl welling up, and hoped that it might counter some of the shapeshifter's influence.

As the others prepared to sleep, Zan wondered whether she would be able to stay awake, but finally decided that there was no reason to keep a watch. If they were being pursued, there was nowhere to run. She closed her eyes and drifted into dreams. She didn't stir again until Ychass woke her with a thought when it was time to move on.

TWELVE

 The Lord of the City was angry. He glared at Hobann with such steeliness that it took all of the merchant's resolve not to cringe. "You told me you would see it done, Hobann," the Lord said, his voice terrible in its quiet fury.

Hobann was not an imposing figure. He was short, for a Vemathen, and rather stout. His pudgy hands, lavishly decked with jewels, waved as he spoke. "My Lord, I did not seek to deceive or disappoint. It was a shock and a blow to me to find that my minstrel . . . objected. From everything the other Khedathi said, I was certain he would take the coward's way out and do as he was bid. I was surprised when he refused, but not alarmed; I believed that he might still be brought to my way of thinking. I never expected him to vanish! Even now, I can't imagine how he got away. My Khedathi beat him to the edge of death."

The Lord tapped his front teeth with his steepled forefingers and regarded the merchant. "It's bad, Hobann — worse than you think. Not only has your minstrel vanished, but the Orathi are gone as well. They disappeared from Efiran's house in the middle of the night, despite the Khedathen guard outside their door."

In spite of his surprise and uneasiness, Hobann had managed to shut his mouth; but at the Lord's next words, it opened with a gasp of shock.

"Efiran's shapeshifter went with them."

"*No*," Hobann breathed, his obsequious manner vanishing as he spun implications behind his hard eyes. "They unchained her; they must have." He barely paused at the Lord's raised eyebrows. "It would explain things — the shapeshifter. What a spy. Who would notice a fly on the wall?"

"It was a risk, though, to unbind her," the Lord said.

Hobann shrugged. "We know very little of the Orathi. Perhaps they are allied with the shapeshifters. Gods know, they think they have little cause to love us."

The Lord struck his fist on the arm of his chair in irritation. "Ah, why wasn't it *you* who met them on the road? Efiran is clever in his way, but . . ." He shook his head. "Ah well, it's no use bewailing what's past. Tell me, Hobann, how do we salvage something out of this shambles?"

"First," Hobann began, allowing none of his inward satisfaction to betray itself, "you must not lose heart. Remember, even if the shapeshifter and my minstrel are with them — which is only supposition, no matter how likely it seems — they still lack Vemathi representation. Further, my minstrel is not likely to be of much use to them with the Wild

130

Khedathi. He was drummed out of his clan for his coward-ice; in fact, I suspect he would be far more of a liability than an asset in a confrontation. Their expedition is still, at best, a chancy one."

"You're not recommending we sit back and wait for them to come to grief, surely? It is very easy to underestimate them."

"I dislike leaving events in the laps of the gods when there is no need to do so, my Lord. There's nothing like the peace of mind a little certainty brings. Send the patrols after them. They're on foot; a thorough sweep on horseback ought to bring them to light. I don't think you'd find a Khedathi patrol that would do them in for you, but if they were brought back to the City, we could remove the threat our-selves."

"How will I explain to the Khedathi? Their notions of honor may prove troublesome."

Hobann shrugged. "Lie. Tell them that my minstrel is believed to have stolen from me, and that the foreigners are implicated in his deed and escape. The Khedathi have a deep contempt for theft and thieves. That ought to suffice."

The Lord of the City began to smile. It was not an attrac-tive expression. "Thank you, Hobann. What would I do without you?"

Hobann permitted himself a little smile. "I'm sure you would manage admirably, my Lord, without my poor aid. One thing more, though: it might be a good idea to keep track of that peculiar daughter of Efiran Moirre, at least until this matter is cleared up. She may have gotten to know them fairly well while they stayed with her family. Gods alone know what motivates the girl, but it wouldn't do to have her . . . *interfere*."

As Remarr had hoped, they reached the first water hole a little before dawn. The spring was meager and muddy, but it was wet, and they were glad of it. There were no caves in which to shelter, so Remarr suggested they pitch their tent in the shade afforded by some stunted vegetation while they waited out the daylight hours. The tent had been designed for four people; with six, it was uncomfortably crowded. After the fourth time Zan got Vihena's elbow in her stomach, she wormed her way to the opening and strung the tent flap up so that it would shade a small scrap of sand for her to sleep on; then she curled up, covering her hands and face with her robe so she wouldn't get sunburned when the sun's position changed. Hours later she woke, cramped and uncomfortable, to find Karivet bending over her. It was time to move on.

Travel in the desert was tiring. The sand, which felt so firm and unyielding when one was trying to sleep, shifted underfoot, making walking heavy work. They were perpetually thirsty, even when their water skins were full, because there was always the chance that they wouldn't find the next spring, or that it would be dry. Twice they saw figures in the distance, but though the sightings alarmed Zan, nothing came of them. Remarr explained that from a distance, their robes covered a multitude of oddities. The Wild Khedathi would not venture far out of their way to investigate strangers unless they had strong reason to believe something was wrong or it seemed that the strangers would be competing for water.

A little after noon on the fourth day, Remarr woke them all. There was worry in his face. "Strike the tent," he said. "We must move on."

"Why?" Karivet asked.

"With my ear to the ground I heard hoofbeats. They are getting close; they must be headed for this water hole. We must be gone before they arrive, or we may be in real trouble. If they are Wild Khedathi, we are in their territory. If it's a patrol from the City —"

"The patrols don't usually come this far," Vihena put in.

"Yes. If it's a patrol, they are looking for us."

They set to work without further discussion. In a surprisingly short time, their gear was packed and they were on their way. As they walked, Zan looked about. There was no sign to indicate they were not the only people on earth. The unrelenting sun pounded down on them, making each step a painful effort, but Remarr kept on, leading them away from the water hole as quickly as he could move them. Suddenly Ychass touched Zan's mind. *Look!*

Behind them, they could see a cloud of dust near the horizon. They were too far away to make out what caused the disturbance, but Remarr looked grave.

"Keep on," he said urgently. "We must be out of sight before they reach the water hole. They are mounted. If they see us, they will be able to overtake us."

The desert air burned in Zan's lungs. Though her mouth

felt dry as sand, she was afraid to stop for even a swallow of water — and the water was too precious to risk spilling by drinking while walking. In the thoughts of her companions she could hear fears and doubts, and Iobeh's desperate desire to keep up with them. Zan reached out her hand to the girl, who took it gratefully.

After what seemed like hours, Remarr called a brief halt, warning them all to drink sparingly.

"I wish we knew whether they made camp at the water hole or pressed on," he said with a sigh. "If they camped, we may be able to elude them."

"I'll find out," Ychass told him. Taking the form of a large hawk, she took to the air. She soared upward for a few minutes, then plummeted earthward in a reckless dive. *They are coming,* she thought to Zan. *Driving their horses hard, too. There are eight of them. Ask Vihena how big patrols are.*

By the time Zan had relayed the information, Ychass was beside them in her woman-form again. "I don't pretend to know anything about weather in the dry lands, but there is a rather nasty-looking yellowish cloud on the western horizon."

Remarr's breath hissed between his teeth in alarm. "Gods! A dust storm. Quickly! Bind your veils over your faces — over your eyes as well; you can see through one or two thicknesses of cloth, and it will keep the sand out of your eyes. Like this." *A rope, too,* he thought as he demonstrated. While he wrapped his veil, Zan unslung her pack and dug out a rope. She looped it once around her waist, then passed it to Ychass. Ychass tied herself in and then helped Iobeh; Iobeh gave it to Karivet, who knotted himself in and handed it to Vihena. When Vihena had tied it around her waist, she gave the last bit to Remarr. His head came up in surprise. He looked very odd with the veil obscuring his features.

"Very good," he said. "Get your veils fixed now. Does anyone need help?" *Is it true, 'Tsan, what they say in the City? You hear thoughts? I know I didn't mention rope aloud.*

She heard the underlying unease in his thoughts. Without allowing her hands to slow in their awkward work of tying her veil, she said aloud, "It's true. I don't do it all the time."

Gods, he thought with vehemence.

"It's a good deal quicker than talking," Ychass pointed out.

"I dare say," he muttered. *I wish I'd known—I wish she'd told me.*

Zan felt a flash of shame. She ought to have confided in him. Before she could apologize, Remarr had turned brisk.

"If everyone's ready," he said, "we'd better move on."

They set off, taking care not to let the rope pull too tightly between them. Zan tried only once to catch Remarr's thoughts; when all she could hear was an intricate piece of music, she took the hint and pulled back from his mind. As they walked, they were aware of two sounds: the keening wind and, much fainter, the muffled thud of distant hooves.

"I wouldn't want to try to take horses into this," Remarr said above the wind. "If we can keep ahead of them until the storm truly breaks, we'll lose them."

Of course, the storm may be harder on us than the Kheda-thi would be, Ychass thought.

Soon the only thing they could hear was the wind. Even with veils across their faces, they could feel the stinging bite of the sand; they wound their sleeves around their hands to keep them from being scoured raw by the storm. Their progress was slower as the storm grew more fierce. Bent almost double against the howling wind, they struggled forward. Karivet stumbled and was hauled to his feet by Vihena.

"We have to find shelter," she shouted. "This will finish us, otherwise."

"Keep on," Remarr boomed back. "We may come to a place where we can rest, but if we stop now, we'll be buried alive."

It grew harder and harder to move. Zan felt the sand collecting in the folds of her robe. It made her feel heavy and leaden. Even with the filtering pieces of cloth over her nose and mouth, she felt there was never quite enough air. It took every bit of her willpower to stay on her feet.

A change in the ground nearly unbalanced her with its steepness. She kept her footing by pure luck and made her way down the side of the dune with care. The wind seemed a little less violent here. Suddenly she found that the others had stopped. Remarr had circled back to face her.

"Do you think we can manage to put the tent up here?" he bellowed. "I don't think we have a chance if we can't. The only person fit for this sort of travel is Vihena — and possibly the shapeshifter. If we put the tent up, we'll have to dig ourselves out when the wind stops, but at least we'll have a chance. Are you game to try?"

"Why not?" she responded. "What's the worst that could happen?"

"We could lose the tent."

"Well, if you're right, we won't need it again if we don't make the attempt." She unslung her pack and dug out the poles. She gave them to Ychass, then got out the tent itself. It took all of them, with much effort, to get the thing anchored. It was lopsided and rather unsteady, but they all managed to get inside. Remarr insisted that they lace the door flap shut before they finally collapsed into exhausted heaps and slept. Outside, the wind moaned around them.

When they woke, the world was silent. It seemed eerie after the noise of the wind. The light inside the tent was dim, too, as though the daylight were weaker in the wake of the storm. As Zan's sleepy mind tried to make sense of that, she noticed Remarr sitting up gingerly. As she watched, he pushed his hand gently against one side of the tent; Zan realized it was bulging inward with the weight of the sand.

"Up," he said quietly. "We'd better dig out before the tent tears. It's not as bad as it could be, but it's bad enough. Help me with the flap."

Fortunately, the flap was on the lee of the dune their tent had caused. They crawled out between two long arms of drifted sand. Remarr showed them where to begin work, and soon they were all busy pushing the sand away from the sides of the tent. When the whole of the tent was exposed, Remarr sat back on his heels and sighed with relief. He unhooked his veil and pushed back his hood, shaking the sand out of it and running his hands through his hair. Iobeh pushed her hood back too, with a smile. Her smile vanished as Remarr's face clouded with concern. She tugged at his sleeve. *What is it? What's wrong?* she signed.

He watched her, at a loss. Ychass came over. "She wants to know what's bothering you."

"It's the storm," he replied, directing his answer to Iobeh. "It wasn't really possible to choose our course, and we've strayed quite a distance from our path."

The others, hearing his voice, had gathered around. "Are we lost?" Karivet asked.

"No," Remarr answered, but there wasn't much reassurance in his tone. "I know where we are, within a few miles. The problem is water. Even before the storm, we were two hard days' journey from the next small water hole. It's closer to three days' journey now, and I don't think we can do it. We can carry only about two days' worth of water. It will mean cruelly short rations."

At the mention of water, Zan felt thirst burn her throat. She forced her voice to remain calm. "If that's the nearest water, we'll just *have* to do it."

"But it's not the nearest water," Remarr admitted unhappily. "There's a nearer spring, maybe four hours from here, but it's a large one. There will almost certainly be Wild Khedathi there."

"We're bound to meet them sooner or later," Vihena said. "We've seen them from a distance already. Surely you weren't expecting to travel through their territory for weeks without meeting them?"

Remarr ignored the scorn in her voice. "Actually, I was hoping just that. The dry lands are vast. We have been following a path few people would take, since we travel on foot, without animals, and toward a destination few people seek."

Vihena sighed. "So you hoped — and your hope has failed. But it's not a matter for such concern. You've said you're a coward, Remarr, but even *you* can't be afraid of them!"

"But I *am* afraid of them, Vihena Moirre — as you would be if you had any sense."

"Don't be stupid. The Khedathi are honorable people — they are *your* people! What can you fear from them?"

Zan heard Remarr's inward struggle with his temper, though none of his anger showed on his face. When he spoke, his voice was patient. "All you know of my people, Vihena Moirre, is based on the Tame Khedathi, the Khedathi who have taken service with Vemathi merchants. Of course the Tame Khedathi are honorable as you understand it; their honor is defined by their masters. The Tame Khedathi have bargained for comfort, and they understand the rules they must observe. In the dry lands the world is different. Honor wears an unfamiliar face. If we found our death at the hands of the Wild Khedathi, it would be not murder in cold blood but an honorable defense of their lands, their water, from outsiders. No doubt you have been told that all Khedathi wish to leave the dry lands. That is not true. The ones who go are a rarity, and they are not much loved by the people they abandon. Khedathi, Wild and Tame, have contempt for defectors."

"What do you recommend?" Zan asked. "Is it really impossible for us to reach the safe spring?"

She heard his thoughts clearly: *I don't think the small ones would survive. The shapeshifter would, and Vihena might. 'Tsan? Gods, who knows? And I? I'd rather risk the desert, but I must think of the others.* "There's no safe choice, 'Tsan," he said at last. "I fear we would not all make it to the small spring."

Zan nodded slowly. "How likely are we to survive an encounter with the Wild Khedathi?"

"I don't know!" Desperation frayed his voice; his thoughts roiled, too turbulent for Zan to read. "But you cannot negotiate with thirst. Of course, we may not be able to negotiate with the Wild Khedathi, either. 'Tsan, you want me to make the decision, but I can't; I dare not."

Zan heard contempt in Vihena's thoughts and rounded on her suddenly. "You needn't be so smug, Vihena," she snapped. "When you don't fully understand what's at stake, decisions are always easy." Vihena recoiled, shocked, and Zan felt suddenly ashamed. She rubbed her face with her hands. "I'm sorry, Vihena, it seems I'm always taking out my ill temper on you. Look, let's get out of the sun while we think about this."

As they crowded into the tent, Karivet got Zan's attention. *Ask me,* he signed. *Perhaps my Gift can resolve the question.*

Zan nodded and began trying to frame her question. She

140

touched his hand and met his eyes. "If we go to the large spring, what will happen?"

"We weave the patterns of our choices on the Loom of Fate," he replied in that eerie, expressionless voice.

Wrong question, Zan thought. *Oh, help.* She tried again. "Which destination gives us the best chance of success, the large spring or the small one?"

"Who can weigh one's life in the balance except oneself?"

Zan bit her lip. Her shoulders were knotted with strain. She couldn't seem to frame the right question. "Can't you tell me anything that would help me decide?" she blurted.

"The smaller spring is dry."

Zan released him, staring in shock. "Oh, Christ," she whispered, beginning to shake as she realized how close she had come to making a disastrous decision. Karivet's face was pale. *The question,* he signed to her. *It has to be the right question.*

"I suppose that settles it," Remarr said. He managed a wry smile for Karivet, which did not mask the sudden bitterness in his thoughts. "You are full of surprises. The gift of prophecy does not grace the Khedathi. I always thought it was a legend."

"I wish it were," Karivet said. "It frightens me. I cannot ask my own questions, and I never know what I am going to say. There are things better left unknown, unspoken, and I cannot choose to keep silent once the question is asked. It is a fearsome responsibility."

"This time," Vihena said bracingly, "you saved our lives."

The look he gave her was bleak. "Perhaps." Iobeh went to

141

him and put her arm around him. The tension gradually eased, replaced by a sense of peace.

Ychass met Zan's eyes. *Are you doing that?* she thought. *I don't want to be soothed.*

It's Iobeh, Zan responded. *Be at peace for her sake.*

The shapeshifter's mind went silent, as though a door had been firmly shut. Zan suppressed a sigh; she was so touchy.

"I think," Remarr said quietly, "we should try to rest. It will be best to come to the water at night. Then there is a chance we can slip in and fill our skins without being seen. Besides, we will not be able to conserve water if we travel by day."

Zan sensed something dark in his thoughts. "Remarr," she began, reaching out to him and touching his arm. He twitched away from her and lay down, turning his back toward her. Zan struggled with her conscience for a moment, but resisted probing him further. With an inward sigh, she tried to settle herself for sleep. Soon she could hear the others' even breathing around her, but sleep eluded her for a long time.

THIRTEEN

Vihena woke them at dusk. In the half-light they took down the tent. After they ate a sparse meal and drank a few sips of water, they stowed their gear and set out. They moved under stars which cast faint light on the vast expanse of sand. Zan looked up at the sky; she still hadn't gotten used to the unfamiliar constellations, though Karivet and Iobeh had begun teaching her some of their names. She saw the Loom, low on the eastern horizon. It made her think of Eikoheh, and she smiled wistfully as she realized how much she missed the old woman. With an effort, she turned her thoughts to matters nearer at hand.

"What are we going to do when we get to the spring? Will the Wild Khedathi be asleep? Can we just sneak up, fill our water skins, and creep away?"

Remarr answered her. "I haven't really thought about it. I can't help hoping there are no Wild Khedathi there. If a clan is camped there, they will have set a guard, even if it is only one person, to watch for storms."

"Hadn't we better make a plan, then?" Zan pressed. "I mean, before we get there? Voices carry so well here."

"Yes, yes. Make a plan." He sounded disgruntled.

"Remarr, you're the only one who knows what the situation is likely to be," she pointed out patiently.

"Do you work magic, Wanderer? Can you put them all to sleep, or make us invisible in their eyes?" he demanded angrily. "How can I make a plan? I don't know what you can do!"

Zan flinched. "I've told you," she insisted. "I hear thoughts — sometimes."

"Yes, and your companions prophesy, change shape, and . . ." His eyes fell on Iobeh. "And gods know what else. And none of this you saw fit to tell me!"

Zan bit her lip. "Look, I'm sorry; I should have told you. I would have, too. I was just waiting —"

He laughed, a jangling, bitter sound. "Don't say waiting for the right moment. We've been traveling nearly a week, Wanderer."

"But I was," she pleaded, hoping for understanding. "In the land of my birth, I am a very ordinary person. I don't have any special gifts or talents; I don't have a destiny or a name out of legend. I'm not used to being so different. I'm not used to my spirit-gift. I should have told you, but I was afraid to. I have enough trouble accepting what is happening to me — how can I share it with anyone?"

Vihena spoke up, her tone philosophical. "She didn't tell me, either, Remarr. You weren't singled out."

"But we are traveling together," he protested. "It is not

right that we have secrets from one another."

"No?" Ychass challenged.

"No. It is not the way of the dry lands to keep secrets from one another."

"How are we to know that? None of us are from the dry lands, Remarr, except you," Karivet pointed out.

"Besides, you have kept secrets from us," Ychass remarked.

"No. I told you I was a coward."

Starlight glinted in Ychass's colorless eyes. "Yes, but you did not tell us you are Outcast, and that a meeting with the Wild Khedathi will probably cost you your life."

Zan bit back a cry of protest. Remarr turned toward her angrily.

"Don't vent your spleen on 'Tsan," Ychass went on. "She didn't tell me this — I took it out of your mind. 'Tsan has scruples. I don't bother with them."

A long look passed between Remarr and the shapeshifter. It took all of Zan's control not to pry.

After a moment Ychass laughed shortly. "Very probably," she remarked. "But listen: if there are people at the spring, I can sneak into their camp and bring water out. No one will notice a night-flying bird, and the guard's attention will be outward. It will take me some time, but it should be safe enough — as safe as anything is, in this game of the Wanderer's. What you should be considering, Remarr, is where we can shelter, come morning."

Ychass, Zan thought at her, *how are you going to carry water if you're a bird?*

When I shift shape, the things I am wearing change, too.

145

There are limits, of course, but a full water skin I can manage.

How — Zan began, but the shapeshifter cut her off sharply.

How do you hear thoughts? It's my people's gift — or curse. I can't explain it. We are the way the gods have made us.

They walked on in silence. After a time a sliver of moon rose, adding only a little to the starlight. They had been walking for several hours when Remarr halted them with a gesture. He pointed, and they saw the glint of light on water. It was a broad pool of silver, set in a small patch of darker ground tucked into a fold between two ridges of pale dunes. Though the oasis was still a mile away, they could see tents like their own crowded around the water. Remarr laid a finger on his lips and gestured in the Khedathi hand-language. Zan found she had no trouble following the thoughts behind the signs, and she translated easily for the twins.

No sound. Noise carries. Can the shapeshifter manage?

Ychass nodded. *Water skin,* she thought to Zan, who gave it to her. The shapeshifter poured the contents of her own skin into Zan's, then slung the empty bag over her shoulder. *I can only take one at a time. Consolidate the contents of the others while I'm gone. Keep your mind open, and I'll tell you if I run into trouble.*

What if you do? What then?

The shapeshifter shrugged. *Call on the gods,* she thought as she became a small bird. Zan followed her flight until she was lost in the darkness.

146

Time slowed, and even their quiet breathing rasped in the silence. Iobeh fidgeted, their anxiety weighing on her. Remarr sat without moving, but Vihena fingered the hilt of her sword. Zan finished emptying all the water skins into one; their contents barely filled it. She laid the four empty skins on the ground before her. When the silence had stretched almost unbearably, Ychass returned. She took her own shape before them, unslung her now full skin, and picked up one of the empty ones. Then she flew off again.

It took a long, tense time, but finally all the skins were full. The group set out again, traveling northwest. Remarr indicated that they must walk briskly if they were to make camp by daybreak. The place he had in mind was a little like Redstone: a deep, dry gully full of rock formations which would hide them from casual eyes. There they could wait out the day, and it was only about a five-hour walk from there to the next small spring. By the time they reached their haven, the sun was just rising. They were too tired to bother with the tent. They found a deep crevice to shelter in and went to sleep.

Early in the afternoon, Zan woke. She found that though the twins and the shapeshifter were still sleeping, Vihena and Remarr were awake. They had moved apart from the others and were talking in low voices. Zan approached them rather diffidently. Remarr was silent, but Vihena greeted her cheerfully.

"Join us, 'Tsan. We haven't enough to do, so we're solving the world's problems in our spare time."

Zan sat down next to her, managing a faint smile for her

joke. "I think I owe both of you an apology."

Vihena shrugged. "If you mean about not telling us about your spirit-gift, I don't blame you. You had no way of knowing whether I was feigning friendship to get information."

"You're generous, Vihena," Zan said. "In any case, I apologize for not telling you both sooner." Her eyes slid, almost unwillingly, to Remarr's inscrutable face. He would not hold her gaze. "What more can I say?" she asked him, pleading.

His dark eyes flicked to her face, then away again. "Nothing. You have apologized. Clearly, your duty is discharged."

"Then why do I feel there's a great gaping well of pain and guilt waiting for me every time I meet your eyes?" she demanded.

He looked at her, startled. "Why should it matter to you?" he asked at last, his voice cool, without inflection.

Vihena looked from one to the other, her eyes full of curiosity. Suddenly Zan felt like a zoo animal. She couldn't stand to meet anyone's eyes; she buried her face in her hands.

"I'm sorry, I'm just not very good at friendship," she muttered. "I don't mean to alienate everyone."

In that same uninflected voice, Remarr said, "Are you listening to my thoughts now?"

"*No!*" She raised her head as the word was torn out of her. Tears filled her eyes.

Remarr's expression came suddenly alive. He reached over to her and gripped her wrist. "Then do — I will never have the courage to say this aloud."

Zan hesitated, fearful in some unnamable way. Then she

reached out with her mind. His thoughts were jumbled, strewn about like flotsam by the intensity of his feelings. She picked up bits, tags of memories, remembered jibes. It was clear that growing up had been hard for him. *I could never learn the Discipline,* she heard him lament. *It wasn't clumsiness, for the harp answers to my touch, but I could never make a blade dance for me. What use a Khedath without a sword?*

She laid her free hand over his and spoke gently. "But didn't you find acceptance among the Vemathi?"

He shook his head, and his thoughts filled with bitterness. *Even my gift of music is ignored. If one's dog speaks, one does not expect it to utter great poetry; one does not listen beyond the marvel. I am so tired of being merely a peculiarity.*

"We're all misfits here," Zan whispered. "Perhaps that means we all belong together."

He merely nodded, but his thoughts elaborated. *That's why it hurt so when I thought you didn't trust me.*

"It wasn't a lack of trust, Remarr, truly — just heedlessness and my own inability to understand or accept my role here. You do believe that, don't you?"

He met her eyes then, and nodded. His smile was like a benediction, and it unknotted some of the tension in her shoulders.

Vihena spoke up into the lightened atmosphere. "If apologies are in order, Remarr, I owe you one, too. Khehaddi tells me it is one of my great failings that I often accept the judgment of others without enough consideration. My friends on the guard do not think well of you — it's because they don't understand you, I think. I fear I've accepted their opinions without considering for myself. I've done you an injustice and I'm sorry for it."

Remarr shrugged. "It's all right. I didn't realize you were friends with Khehaddi Ontarr. I respect her — she thinks with more than her blade."

Fierce enthusiasm animated Vihena's face. "Khehaddi's wonderful. She taught me everything I know, but even more than that, she took me seriously when no one else would. You can't imagine how important that was for me. It made life bearable." She sighed, shaking her head a little sadly. "Mother has always maintained that I could find a husband by learning to make myself indispensable, but I couldn't do it. I could never even pretend interest in household things. The Khedathi fascinated me: the way the women walk about as free as men, able to do what they want. And the swordplay is so beautiful — like dance, only deadly. I used to loiter near the barracks and the training grounds whenever I could. For the most part the Khedathi ignored me; a few taunted me. But Khehaddi noticed me, and she listened to me. And then she agreed to teach me the Discipline."

Zan's gaze crossed Remarr's, and they shared a rueful smile, each recognizing the envy in the other's face.

"In some ways I'm closer to Khehaddi than to my own family. She understands me — who I really am, not who I ought to be — better than I understand myself sometimes. And she cares about me." Her eyes softened with memory.

150

"She told me once that she would be proud to claim me for a daughter." She smiled. "I guess that sounds maudlin, but you can't imagine how important it was at the time."

"I can," Zan said softly, her voice catching on tears. "I wish my father had said such a thing even once." Memory flashed bitter, then poignant: her father's face, abstracted, a fountain pen pushed up against his teeth. She realized how much it hurt her to know that now he would never look up from his work, find her eyes, and say the words she longed to hear.

"I envy you, Vihena," Remarr said, "as mean-spirited as that sounds. Khehaddi is a mentor anyone would be proud to have."

They lapsed into a companionable silence until Ychass and the twins woke, a short time later, and they all prepared to move on.

For several days after that, everything went smoothly. As Remarr had explained, this was the easiest leg of the journey. The springs were fairly close together, and water was not a pressing problem. Though a couple of the springs beside which they camped were very low, none was actually dry. At one of their campsites, Remarr managed to snare a small desert animal called a *nihekh,* which looked a little like a prairie dog, and they had a warm meal that afternoon for the first time. The stew Remarr made was tasty, and they ate every bit of it.

It was a peaceful time, especially late in the day, after everyone had slept and before they were ready to set off on their evening's hike. Remarr and Vihena made rapid progress with the twins' hand-language, and often Remarr sang for them or told them a story. Even the shapeshifter seemed to enjoy the stories, though she didn't much care for the singing. Zan began to relax; she began to believe that the patrols had given up looking for them, and as they never saw anyone, even from a distance, it became easy — fatally easy — to believe themselves the only people in the dry lands.

One afternoon, as they sat in the long shadow cast by the tent, Remarr looked up from tuning his harp. "Do your people sing, 'Tsan?"

Zan thought briefly of hard rock and grimaced. "Sometimes."

"Teach me one of their songs."

She blinked, at a loss. But she could see his eagerness, so she racked her brain for something suitable. "Well," she said finally, "I could teach you a — a —" She settled on the English word. "Round. The words are easy, they just repeat over and over. *Dona nobis pacem*. It means 'give us peace.'"

He repeated the words, struggling a little over the *-cem*. Vihena moved a little closer. "May I learn, too?"

Karivet also wanted to be taught, and soon they were engrossed. Remarr was amazingly quick, Karivet had a pleasant voice and a good ear, but Vihena was the real surprise. She had a rich contralto voice, well trained. Remarr raised his eyebrows at her, and to Zan's surprise she blushed.

"You've studied singing," he said.

She nodded unhappily. "I couldn't even do *that* right. My voice is too low for a woman."

"It's unusual," he told her.

"It's *beautiful!*" Zan exclaimed. "It would make your fortune in the land of my birth. But never mind. There are three parts to this song; here's the second."

In a short time they were all singing. The sound floated out, lovely though strangely out of place in the vastness of the desert. Remarr picked up his harp and began playing along with them. When they tired of singing, he played on alone, improvising on the simple tunes and harmonies Zan had given him. Finally even the harp's voice succumbed to the silence. Remarr set his harp aside, then met Zan's eyes and smiled.

"Tomorrow you can teach us another song, if you will."

"I shouldn't think, Outcast, you'll be needing any more songs," a new voice said, "unless they sing in the Shadow Lands."

Remarr turned his head, then froze as he found the point of a sword in his face. His gaze traveled up the length of steel to the brown hand that held it, then to the cold eyes of the veiled Khedatheh who held it.

"Get up. Meet your death on your feet."

"I am unarmed," he said quietly.

"Do you think that will save you? *You are Outcast!*"

As he started to get to his feet, Vihena leapt up, her sword whispering from its sheath. "He may be unarmed, but I'm not." Her blade knocked the other aside with a metallic ring. Remarr rolled backward out of reach and got up.

The Khedatheh faced Vihena. "Do you challenge me for an Outcast? You cannot hope to save him — his life is forfeit. Put up your blade or it will go hard with you."

Vihena did not answer, merely remained standing with

her blade at the ready. The Khedatheh whistled shrilly and other Khedathi rose out of the dunes and approached, waiting beyond the edge of the camp.

"Yield him to us," the Khedatheh said, "and we will allow you to go your way."

Zan rose, pushing back her hood so that her red hair blazed against her white robe. "If you take him from us, you have killed us all, for we do not know the desert."

The Khedatheh's eyes widened, and Zan heard her thoughts clearly. *Curse it! Now that the others have seen, I can't let them go.* "You are Outlanders! What are you doing in the dry lands?" There was outrage in her tone.

"We travel to Windsmeet to ask a boon of the gods," Zan said, more calmly than she felt.

The woman stared at her, and Zan was hard put not to flinch at the force of her reaction. *Windsmeet! And with my cowardly son? No! It cannot be true.* She rounded on Vihena. "Is that true?"

"Yes."

The woman's eyes narrowed suddenly. "I have never seen a Khedatheh with gray eyes. Who are you?"

Vihena put back her own hood, without lowering her sword. "I am Vihena Moirre."

"Vematheh!" The Khedatheh spoke as though the word soiled her mouth. "Since when have the pampered women of the merchants taken up arms?"

Vihena's smile was mirthless. "Not all of them — only me. My father says I am one of the gods' jokes, since I was born on the Feast of the Trickster."

154

The intensity of the mental reactions to that statement made both Ychass and Zan wince, and Iobeh buried her face in her hands. *Gods! Gods!* It was the Khedatheh and Remarr both; they had the same stricken look on their faces. Then thoughts began tumbling about furiously. Out of this intense jumble, one stream of thought prevailed, the Khedatheh's. *I've said it; I never believed it; but oh, merciless gods, it's true! Changelings! They're both changelings.*

The Khedatheh sheathed her sword and made the welcoming gesture. Vihena returned it, bafflement clear on her face and in her mind.

"My name is Emirri of clan Khesst. I am the clan leader. I bid you welcome, foster kin."

"F-foster kin?" Vihena repeated. "But I don't understand." Clear in her thoughts was amazement. Not even Khehaddi had openly claimed foster kinship with her, though she had come close. That perfect strangers, the Wild Khedathi whom Remarr so feared, would do so was unthinkable.

Gods! Ychass thought. *Hasn't she any more sense than to go questioning a colossal piece of luck like this?*

Emirri shook her head slowly. "Small wonder that you do not. I barely do myself." She gestured with her chin toward Remarr. "He was born also on the Feast of the Trickster — and it would seem the Trickster had her way with you both." She shook her head again. "Is it not true that the City women are meek, that they do no work that could callous their smooth and scented hands? I have never heard of even one who learned the Discipline. Even your own father calls you a joke of the gods. From everything you say, you are as foreign to the clan of your birth as he is to us." She gestured toward Remarr with her chin again. "He would or could not learn the Discipline, but preferred to spend his time with that City toy of his. Here the Discipline is like water: it is part of life. You cannot choose to do without it and survive. He was so strange to us that we could only explain him as a changeling, and finally we cast him out to find his way among the people to whom his spirit belongs. You . . ." She hesitated, meeting Vihena's eyes squarely. "You have the fierce spirit that should have been his, as he has yours, at the will of the wise and inscrutable gods. For this reason, my clan will honor you as kin, and for your sake we will welcome your companions. We will even tolerate the Outcast, since it is through him that you have been made known to us. Give me the names of your friends so that I may present them to my people."

While Vihena complied, somewhat dazedly, Zan sent her own puzzlement to Ychass. *I don't understand. How can this Emirri leap to such a conclusion? They might not even have been born in the same year.*

The Feast of the Trickster comes only once in twenty-one years, Ychass returned. *I have heard that the Khedathi are extremely superstitious. This must be an instance of it.*

But would *the gods meddle like that?* Zan insisted. *I mean, mixing two spirits . . . ?*

Who knows? The mental shrug was strong. *But of them all, the Trickster would be most likely. And this mixing sounds like the sort of thing that would amuse her. She is most unpredictable, and uses her power without principles. That is why her feast comes so seldom. It is all the other gods can do to limit her power.*

Zan shivered. It unnerved her to hear someone thinking of the gods as real and active, as having personalities, even if unpredictable ones. Somehow she had never gotten as far as thinking of the gods as real beings. Even though the purpose of their quest was to achieve the gods' intervention, Zan had somehow managed to shy away from that aspect of it; it was very easy to concentrate on getting to Windsmeet without considering what would happen when they got there.

Suddenly her musings were cut off, as she found herself being presented to the clan leader and her escort. If the truth be told, she was grateful to be distracted from her thoughts.

FOURTEEN

The shuttle hissed through the warp as the treadles thudded under Eikoheh's feet. The Fate grew on the loom, full of the golds and whites of the desert. Ohmiden watched anxiously. There had been a moment when he feared Eikoheh would lose that one strand of vibrant blue, but now she seemed to have it under control. There was strain in the weaver's face as she laid her life in the pattern. It was hard work, Ohmiden knew, and this was worse than most, since there were so many strands and shades to keep sorted. He waited until it seemed Eikoheh had reached a calm place, then he spoke quietly.

"I've made supper."

She laid the shuttle aside and brushed her hair out of her face. "How domestic of you," she jibed. "More rabbit stew?"

"No, chicken. And some fresh spinach. You're working too hard."

She fixed him with a sharp look. "Whose idea was it that

158

I weave a Fate, anyway? Ohmiden, it's difficult for me. There's more going into it than I understand or can control, and if it gets away from me, I can't imagine what will happen. I can't escape the Fate — even my dreams are full of the desert." She shook her head. "Sometimes I imagine the merciless gods watching me and laughing: 'Look at that old fool of a weaver — she thinks she can weave a Fate with the gods in it.' It was stupid to begin, but it would be disastrous to stop." With a sigh, she got up from the loom and went to her cushions by the hearth. "Gods, I wish I knew whether I am doing the right thing!"

Ohmiden ladled thick stew into a bowl and handed it to her before he answered. "You will not know that, Eikoheh, until we know whether or not the young ones succeed. You cannot judge the pattern until the cloth is finished."

"Yes. And when one is weaving Fates, one cannot stop to unravel." She was silent, eating, her face drawn in lines of worry and exhaustion. After a while she looked up at Ohmiden. "Tomorrow I will need three new colors. Will you wind the shuttles for me? I'm bone weary."

He nodded. "Colors?"

She shrugged. "You choose them. I can't even see straight, much less think."

They finished their meal and Eikoheh stumbled off to bed. Ohmiden watched her go, then rose and went to the shelf where Eikoheh kept her yarns. He chose carefully, letting his inner eye, the part that dreamed, influence him. He brought the lamp over and set it beside his cushions before beginning the tedious task of winding yarn onto the

159

wooden shuttles. The lamp had guttered low before he finished.

They were welcomed into the clan. It seemed incredible to Zan that this tangle of weird coincidences could be accepted and turned into such an explanation, but it was so. Not only were they accepted, but Emirri and the other clan elders decided to accompany the little band of foreigners through the dry lands to Windsmeet.

"The deep desert is no place for a clutch of untried youngsters," Emirri told Vihena. "We would be failing our kin duty to you if we allowed you to go off so ill prepared. We will not go onto Windsmeet with you, for it is not laid upon us to tempt the gods, even for kin, but we will see to it that you arrive there, if it is within our power."

The clan Khesst was a large one, including many people and a good number of clean-limbed, desert-bred horses. Iobeh awed the horsemaster, a grizzled Khedathen named Shokhath, by befriending a notoriously difficult mare. She spent a great deal of time with the animal, but her triumph was complete the day she rode past a crowd of Khedathi on its back. She used no saddle nor bridle, but guided the mare by the gentle pressure of her hands on either side of the horse's neck. Shokhath spent much of the next few days with Iobeh, trying to fathom the secret of her success. Zan enjoyed watching their "conversations"; Iobeh was very inventive in her efforts to make the man understand her.

While they traveled with the clan Khesst, Zan noticed that Remarr and Ychass both kept themselves apart. She could understand Ychass's reasons — Zan could hear the uneasiness and suspicion in the Khedathi's thoughts; they were not comfortable with a shapeshifter in their midst, although they tolerated her for Vihena's sake — but Remarr's attitude puzzled her. It was not that the clan did not trust him; they did not seem to think of him at all. When she tried to ask him about it, he cut her questions off brusquely and began avoiding her as well. So Zan shook her head and watched.

She saw a great deal. Vihena seemed to be entirely in her element. She had been easily accepted by the younger members of the clan, even to the point of sparring with them in their daily training bouts. Zan also saw that Vihena had taken Karivet under her wing; she and her new friends were teaching him to handle the Khedathi throwing dagger. He showed an aptitude for it that surprised them all.

Zan herself spent much of her time in the company of Fiorreh, the clan storyteller. Fiorreh was a tiny old woman whose hair was bleached bone white by age and the sun, and whose dark, mischievous eyes were set in a face seamed with wrinkles. She had a wonderful voice, rich and compelling, that seemed completely at odds with her delicate appearance. She was an amusing companion, always with an explanation or an anecdote on her lips. Once Zan asked her if a particularly outrageous story was really true, and Fiorreh laughed.

"I'm a storyteller, Stranger — I am not bound by the truth.

Besides, the explanations I give are so interesting they *should* be true. And they would be, if the gods had thought of them."

One day, when they had been traveling for nearly a week, the clan was overtaken by a group of mounted Khedathi. As Fiorreh watched them approach, she told Zan to fasten the veil she had let fall open.

"This could be trouble," the old woman said. "They are Tame."

"How can you tell from this distance?" Zan asked.

Fiorreh shrugged. "The horses. They are wearing too much metal to be Wild. Metal is scarce here, Stranger. We use it for swords; we don't waste it on ornaments for animals."

A few minutes later, the truth of Fiorreh's words was borne out. The head of the patrol dismounted and approached Emirri. "I am Shohandeh of clan Nikhett," the Tame Khedatheh said. "We are looking for foreigners. We have reason to believe they have entered your territory."

Emirri's answer nearly stopped Zan's heart. "Indeed, there are foreigners in my territory," she said deliberately. "They stand in front of me, Shohandeh of . . . the City." She folded her arms across her chest. "You do not have leave to hunt our lands or to drink our water."

Shohandeh made a placating gesture. "You do not understand. These foreigners are thieves without honor. There are six of them: two from the forest, small — children; one from the City; one Outcast from the dry lands; one who is of the vile kindred that shifts shape; and one, with hair like fire,

162

from gods alone know where. Have you seen them?"

"You said they are thieves. What have they stolen?"

The patrol leader shrugged. "I do not know. Some merchant's thing. Have you seen them?"

"I will tell you this: besides yourselves, I know of no people in our territory who do not belong here. You and your company do not have leave to hunt our lands or to drink our water. Go hence before we lose our patience."

"We would count it a tremendous favor, clan leader, if you would permit my people to see the faces of your clan uncovered."

"I see no reason to show you any more favor than I have already. We have not cut you to pieces. Be thankful and go."

"At least tell me what clan this is so that I may report to my overlord."

Emirri's tone was full of contempt. "Khesst," she said curtly.

Zan felt the startled reaction of the spokeswoman. *That's the coward's clan; they wouldn't shelter him.* Shohandeh turned and walked back to her mount. A moment later the patrol wheeled their animals and went back the way they had come.

Emirri shook her head, then turned to Zan. "What did you steal, Stranger, that the Tame Dogs come nosing into the dry lands after you?"

"We did not steal anything, clan leader. But the City people do not want us to ask our boon of the gods."

Emirri's dark eyes were inscrutable, but her thoughts were clear. *How can I trust them not to bring dishonor on us?*

163

"Stranger," she said warningly, "even Tame Khedathi do not lie."

"No, but surely they can be misled. The only thing we can be said to have taken from the City that was not given to us is your son, and we only took him because he was unable, at the time, to bring himself."

Emirri's eyes narrowed. "My son?"

Zan felt a sick uneasiness. She knew she had heard Emirri call Remarr "son" in her thoughts, but she couldn't remember whether anyone had said it aloud. She hesitated for a moment, then decided to brazen it out. "Am I mistaken, then? Remarr is not your son?"

The clan leader's voice was soft, full of suspicion. "He is, Stranger, but it occurs to me to wonder how you know."

"He told me once," Zan replied carefully, "that his mother had always insisted he was a changeling. When you called him that, it seemed a logical conclusion to reach."

Emirri was silent for a long moment. Her thoughts were agitated, and none of it made any sense to Zan. Finally she spoke. "And you are not a thief."

"I am not."

"Stranger, I do not own him as my son, nor do I speak his name."

Zan saw Remarr in her mind's eye, standing apart and lonely. "You are hard," she said quietly.

"There is no room for softness in the dry lands," Emirri retorted grimly. "Why do you think I cast him out?" She turned abruptly and walked away.

Zan stared after her for a moment, her lips pressed tightly

together. Then she sighed. Beside her, Fiorreh laid her hand on Zan's arm. "Do not judge the clan leader too harshly, Stranger. Our ways are not yours. And she was so disappointed in him." The storyteller gestured toward Remarr, who was standing yards away from anyone else. "His father died a month before he was born. Emirri truly loved Tekharr, and she was deeply grieved at his death. She was pleased to have borne a son, for she believed he would live out the promise Tekharr had shown. She told us all her son would be the best warrior, the greatest clan leader. We got very tired of hearing it, but we listened because we felt pity for her grief. Later, when everyone could see how inept he was, how the blades would not answer him, how he could not master the Discipline, she remembered her boasting and was humiliated. She never forgave herself." The old woman spread her hands. "Or him."

"It hardly seems fair," Zan remarked.

"None of it is fair," Fiorreh said with vehemence. "It is not fair that Tekharr died before he saw the face of his son. It is not fair that Emirri was left behind to raise him. It is not fair that she never found any other man to love, and that she will leave the clan without a child of her line. And it is not fair that he has returned to remind her of old hurts. None of it is fair, Stranger. The gods do not care about fairness!"

"Then why are we going to Windsmeet to ask the gods to prevent an injustice?"

The old woman tipped her head to one side and regarded Zan with bright, dark eyes. "What else can you do, Stranger?"

As Zan watched the old woman walk off, she felt Ychass's presence in her mind. *Doubts?*

Yes, Zan replied, quickly filling the shapeshifter in on her conversation with the storyteller.

Gods are fickle and merciless, 'Tsan. It is a sad fact. But we have nothing else on which to put our hopes. This whole venture has been hopeless from the start, but that didn't stop you from beginning. Don't let it trouble you now.

FIFTEEN

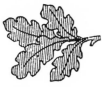Efiran Moirre was startled when he saw Captain Khehaddi's sun-darkened face. He hailed her. "I didn't expect to see you here — I thought you were on patrol."

She nodded. "We got in early this morning. Are you well? How is Vihena?"

Efiran's heart froze. "Wasn't she with your patrol?" The words choked him.

The captain's eyes narrowed with concern. "Indeed, no. Did — did you think she was?"

He nodded, his voice failing him utterly.

"You haven't seen her in the whole time the patrol was out of the City?"

He nodded again.

"Merciless gods!" the Khedatheh breathed. "Efiran, where could she be?"

"She must have gone with them."

"Gone with *whom?*"

167

He looked at her nervously. "With the Stranger, and the Orathi — to Windsmeet."

Khehaddi's face went still. She remembered some of the garbled talk of the barracks: thieves, an outcast, something stolen from Hobann. And now, Vihena involved. She would have to get to the bottom of this. She turned on her heel and set off toward the barracks in a long-legged lope. She didn't even hear Efiran's anxious query behind her.

She reached the barracks as another dusty patrol rode up. It was Shohandeh's; they looked tired. Khehaddi listened from the edges of the group that had gathered to welcome them. Belerann stood in the center, his face grave as he listened to Shohandeh.

"— didn't find any sign of them. Most of the clans were helpful, and even unveiled. Khesst wouldn't, but that didn't surprise me — they have a reputation for being standoffish. But I'm not worried about them. They are the minstrel's clan. They'd never shelter him."

"You did well," Belerann said quietly. "Go rest while I speak to Hobann and the Lord to see what plan they have now."

"The Orathi *must* be dead," another Khedathen volunteered. "That storm — Edevvi lost two seasoned veterans in it. A group of wetlanders couldn't have survived."

Argument and speculation began as Belerann moved off. Khehaddi intercepted him as he left the other Khedathi behind. "A word," she said softly.

He raised his eyebrows and nodded.

"What was it that Hobann said they stole from him?"

168

His brows knit. "I don't believe he said — some merchant's thing."

"Worth Khedathi lives?"

He shrugged. "What of theirs is, besides the rain?"

"Belerann, Vihena Moirre is with them."

He drew a sharp breath, then let it out slowly. "Not thieves, then. Khehaddi, don't ask any more questions."

"How can I be silent? Hobann is lying to us. There is no honor in hiding from the truth."

"What can it matter now? Surely they are dead."

"You don't believe that," she retorted, "or you would not be trying to silence me. If they are not thieves, Belerann, we *cannot* go on hunting them. Honor forbids —"

The Khedathen gripped her arm and shook it. "Softly! You have not thought it through." His tone gentled to persuasion. "Khehaddi, think: you have, what, another five years of active service? Then what? Will you go back to clan Ontarr in the dry lands?" She gave a baffled choke of protest as he hurried on. "No, of course not. You will settle on a farm, with your sons. But wait, think: what if there are no lands? If the gods grant these meddling children their boon, Khehaddi, where will you go? What will you do? And in any case, it is not as though we will harm the Orathi when we clear the forests."

For an instant she stared at him in astonishment. Then her lips twisted as she hissed, "Is honor *dead?* You gave your *word!*"

"I promised them we would wait. I never said we would not interfere."

Bitterness seeped into her expression, staining her tone. "You have lived here too long, Belerann — you are thinking like a merchant. What you propose is murder. Though we may not do the deed, their blood will be on our hands."

"We swore oaths to the Vemathi to protect their interests. Surely that is all we are doing."

"It is not, and you know it!"

Belerann was silent for a long time, staring into the challenge in Khehaddi's eyes. Tension flickered between them like fire. Finally he made the gesture conceding a touch, but he did not release her gaze. "You speak the bitter truth, Khehaddi — what we are doing is not honorable. Nonetheless, the guidance of our people is in my hands, and I will not change our course. You have the right to challenge me, if you choose."

A spasm of pain crossed her features; he spoke of battle to the death, and they had been friends a long time. "*Why?*" she demanded, the cry reft from her silence.

His gaze turned inward for a moment, as though he were rehearsing the twists and turns of his decision. When he spoke, his voice was distant, but touched with sadness. "I have grown accustomed to rain."

His words sparked a vivid memory of the rain-washed City, rich with the fresh green scent of spring, gleaming against the pink and gold sunset. With a pang, Khehaddi realized the depth of the sacrifice her honor asked. She hesitated, and in that instant realized that she couldn't do it. If she challenged him, she would lose, for her heart was torn, and Belerann was good enough to demand her total concentration. She railed inwardly at her weakness, but against her will, her gaze dropped. "As have I," she whispered, "gods curse it." She looked up then, suddenly, the flash of resolution back in her eyes. "But I will not have Vihena Moirre harmed."

For an instant he looked doubtful. He opened his mouth to argue with her, but he thought better of it and merely shook his head slightly. "I will send you with the company that goes to Windsmeet, then, to see that she is not."

Travel with clan Khesst was faster than they could have managed on their own — and more comfortable. Each day, late in the afternoon, they would break camp, load the horses, and set out. They set a rapid pace to the next spring, made camp, and slept out the rest of the night. The clan arose early in the morning, and rested again when the sun was at its zenith. Once she got used to the odd hours, Zan enjoyed the travel. Riding was not as exhausting as walking, so she found she needed less sleep. The days passed quickly as the miles spun away under the horses' hooves.

Toward the end of the second week, a dawn came when they could see Windsmeet's sand-scoured bulk hunched against the horizon. It was a hill of dark stone, its top scraped flat by the merciless storms. It looked unnatural, lacking even a shadow of vegetation, and so much darker than the surrounding sand.

As Zan stood looking at it, Vihena came to summon her

to Emirri's tent for a council. It did not improve Zan's state of mind to find that of the foreigners, only she and Vihena were present.

"We have brought you as far as the clan as a whole may go," Emirri told them. "There is a spring, a small one, nearer to Windsmeet, but there is not enough water there for all my people and our animals. I will give you horses if you wish it, but . . ." She shrugged. "It is a small spring, and they drink a great deal. It will not take you a night's travel, even on foot, to reach the spring, and from there it is perhaps two hours to the top of Windsmeet."

Zan nodded.

"We will wait for you — three days. By then the gods will have answered, if they are going to. If you return to us, we will guide you out of the desert. If you stay longer than three days —" she made a gesture with one hand — "you are on your own. Is that understood?"

"It is, and it is most generous of you, Emirri," Zan replied. "I do not think we will require horses. We will set out to-night, if you think it advisable."

"None of this venture is advisable, Stranger, if you ask me. I think it is no more foolish for you to start tonight than for you to wait, however. My people are uneasy in the shadow of Windsmeet."

"I thank you, foster mother, for your aid," Vihena said. "Without your help we would at best still be wandering the dry lands leagues from here, and at worst we would be dead, or under guard in the City."

172

"It was my kin duty," Emirri said.

Vihena bowed her head in acknowledgment, but Zan heard the underlying thought, that kin duty did not usually include sheltering outcasts and foreigners. Zan also murmured her thanks as Emirri dismissed them. Once outside, she went in search of the others, while Vihena went off with her friends.

Remarr proved the most elusive of Zan's companions, but she finally ran him to earth in the tent they shared. He had his harp in his hands but was not playing. When she came in, he laid it aside and looked up at her.

"Emirri thinks we should set out tonight," she told him. "The clan will wait three days for us. Remarr, you must know some stories — what usually happens to people who ask boons of the gods?"

He shrugged. "There's no 'usually,' 'Tsan. All the stories are different."

She sat down on the floor of the tent. "I bet they don't go home and live happily ever after, though."

"No. But it's too late to worry about that, surely?"

She sighed and nodded. "But Remarr, can't you tell me what we might expect?"

He spread his hands. "Expect the unexpected. 'Tsan, it all depends on which of the gods answers — if in fact any does."

"So what are the choices? The only god I've heard named is the Trickster. There must be others."

"Indeed, yes. There are many, many of them: the Weaver, the Mother, the Namegiver, the Warrior, the Dreamer, the

Harvester — those are a few only. If I had to choose, I'd want the Weaver, or possibly the Dreamer. According to the tales, they are two of the gentler ones."

"Is it random, the selection of the god?" she pursued.

He shrugged eloquently. "All this speculation is fruitless, unless it serves to reassure your mind, 'Tsan. To tell you the truth, I don't believe we'll even know which god answers us, unless we are told."

That rocked Zan backwards. She blinked at him in surprise. "You mean you won't recognize them? But they are your gods! Don't you have pictures of them or something in your —" She stopped dead, at a loss. She had never heard a word for temple.

Remarr cocked his head at her. "In the land of your birth, then, do you have portraits of your gods?"

"No," she protested, exasperated. "But my God doesn't appear in a specific place to answer questions, either."

"You have only one god? Your land must be very strange."

She laughed suddenly as she tried to imagine Remarr and the others fitting in in Manhattan. "I believe you would find it so," she agreed.

"Do you have a City?"

"Oh, there are many cities, and they are large, much larger than your City. They are full of tall, tall towers, and roads, and people, and they are dirtier than the City and far more crowded. They can be dangerous, especially at night."

"Why? Are there wild beasts?"

She smiled ruefully. "In a sense. There are some people

174

who will steal from you, and a very few who seem to love violence for its own sake."

"Do they scorn honor? Or do they not understand it?"

Zan was silent, frowning as she pondered that. "I think," she said at last, "that most people like to think they're honorable, but they are not always willing to take the risks that acting honorably requires."

"That sounds like hypocrisy."

"Yes, and it is fueled by greed and self-interest. But it's not all bad, Remarr — there are good things, too." She paused briefly, trying to cast her description in terms he would understand. "There are places where precious and beautiful things are kept so that many people can see them, and great centers of learning where many people go to study. There are vast markets, where one can buy almost anything. There are places you can go to hear music, and places you can go to see strange animals. It is easy to travel quickly from one region to another, and there are ways to talk with people who are far away." She shook her head, laughed. "This is hard; I can't explain."

"Do you miss it?"

She was silent for a moment, then she shook her head. "I don't think I do. There's nothing to draw me back there, Remarr. My father is dead; I have no family. I've never had friends before — at least, not ones like you and the others. There are things that I miss" (*like books,* she thought to herself), "but on the whole, I am content here." As she looked at his intent face, a sudden suspicion kindled in her mind and she narrowed her eyes at him. "Of course," she added, "I would be *more* content if I knew what was going to happen tonight."

He looked up at her, startled, then smiled and made a slight conceding gesture in her direction. "It couldn't last. It's true, I was trying to divert your attention, 'Tsan, but what you were telling me is fascinating. I would very much enjoy hearing more about your land. Perhaps one day you could tell me some of the tales of your people."

She didn't feel up to explaining about books and libraries, so she merely nodded. Remarr stowed his harp in its case and rose, slinging the strap over his shoulder. As he started for the opening, she called his name and he paused, looking back at her curiously. "Thank you," she said.

He smiled, and in reply offered her an elaborately graceful court bow. Then he was gone. She sighed deeply, then smiled to herself as she realized that though her worry was still there, it no longer gnawed at her peace of mind quite so hungrily.

SIXTEEN

The rest of the journey to Windsmeet was uneventful. They arrived at the foot of the hill a little before moonrise. To Zan's surprise, there was a track that led them in generous switchbacks to the crest of Windsmeet. As they came to the top of the hill, the moon cleared the horizon, so that each of them was silhouetted against its pale disk. In their desert robes they looked peculiarly similar; it gave Zan an uneasy feeling.

"Now what do we do?" she asked to cover her nervousness. To her annoyance, her voice came out as a whisper.

"I suppose we call on the gods for justice," Remarr whispered back. "Shall I do it?"

"No," Karivet said quickly. "I will. It is on behalf of my people that we have come." The others acquiesced, but Iobeh went to his side and took his hand. Karivet straightened his shoulders and raised his voice. "Gods! Gods, hear me. We have come, representatives of every kindred, to ask your aid. Hear us. Answer us."

His voice sounded tiny in the emptiness. For a moment there was no sound except the companions' quiet breathing, then a blast of harsh wind swept across the mesa. They covered their faces with their veils and shut their eyes to keep out the dust. When the wind died and they opened them again, they found themselves facing a tall figure, dark against the moon.

"You have summoned me." It was a woman's voice, cool, almost disdainful, but full of assurance and power. "What boon do you seek, child of the forest?"

Karivet took a deep breath, tightening his grip on Iobeh's hand. With the god's face in shadow, it was hard to tell anything about her; he could not read her mood from her voice alone. "The people of the City and the people of the desert between them have determined to wrest a vast tract of the forest from my folk. Since we do not bear arms against other peoples, we have no recourse but to appeal to you. We ask you to intercede on our behalf, to stop these stronger peoples from doing as they will despite the consequences to my people. We were told they would abide by the gods' decision. We beseech your aid, and we await your decree."

The silence stretched long. Zan could feel her heart thudding rapidly against her ribs.

Finally the god raised one hand, palm upward, and spoke. "You ask my help. What will you give me in return? Surely my help is worth something to you."

Karivet swallowed hard. "What could we have that would be of value to you?"

The outstretched hand clenched and her voice went suddenly cold. "I could ask you for a life, for example."

At that, Iobeh dropped her brother's hand and knelt before the god. Zan sprang forward and grasped the girl by the shoulders. "Iobeh, no!" She looked up at the dark figure. "Name something else," she demanded.

The god laughed; it was an uncomfortable sound. "I did not say I *would* ask you for a life, only that I could. And I will not, though you may come to regret that. I will set you a quest. It will be dangerous — it could well cost all of your lives — but it will spare your consciences. Go to my brother who dwells in the teeth of the winds; ask him for a flask of the snows' blood and bring it here to me. Only then will I consider the judgment you desire. I have spoken. You will have no other word from me." The god vanished in another blast of wind and dust.

They looked at one another helplessly. "The teeth of the winds?" Karivet repeated. "How are we to find *that?*"

There was silence until Ychass answered. "That is the name of some mountains far to the north of here. The Snowsblood is a river that originates in them."

Zan heard the unease in the shapeshifter's mind and probed. *How dangerous a journey?*

It will take the Trickster's own luck to survive at all, Ychass thought grimly. *We will have to cross my people's land. The Wild Khedathi and the desert are child's play by comparison.*

How can that be? Zan replied, adding, with a weak attempt at humor, *Surely after all this time you aren't going to tell me your people really do drink the blood of infants.*

The shapeshifter did not reply, in thought or words, but Vihena spoke. "North," she said. "But that's through the shapeshifters' land. We can't go there."

"Why not?" Zan demanded.

"Because of the tribute," Vihena explained. "The shapeshifters pay tribute so that no one will enter their lands or interfere with their people."

Zan turned to Ychass. "Well, isn't there someone whose permission we could ask? After all, it's not as though we were planning to settle there; we just want to pass through."

Ychass spread her hands. "Perhaps they would listen to you, 'Tsan; I don't know. I cannot negotiate for you — they would kill me before they would speak with me." There was an ocean of bitterness in her voice. "They took my name, they cast me out of the Temple, they bound me in silver, and they gave me to the Vemathi. It was not a kindness to give me to the City people in my own shape; it was the cruelest fate they could devise to send me, aware and helpless, into far lands. I am worse than outlawed to them, worse than dead — they made me *chiasst,* unchanging. It will not reassure them to find me restored, and in the company of foreigners. They will assume that I have returned for revenge." Her eyes narrowed and her lips curved in a humorless smile. "And I am not sure they would be wrong."

Zan caught Vihena's stray thought: *She sure knows how to make friends.*

Ychass turned on her, her pale eyes gleaming in the

moonlight. "I don't need friends," she hissed. "Friendship is a fable that survives only among people who are crippled, weak, deaf to thoughts."

Zan caught Ychass's arm. "I am not deaf to thoughts, as you know, and I am your friend."

"You!" Ychass laughed. "You are outside of every category, Stranger."

Zan recoiled as though the shapeshifter had struck her, and she closed her mind off with as much force as she could manage.

Beside her, Remarr spoke up. "Isn't there a way to avoid most of the shapeshifters' land? Perhaps if we angle west and then north?"

Ychass shook her head. "Not if we hope to find the source of the Snowsblood. The Teeth of the Winds run east and west for hundreds of miles, and no one knows how far they stretch to the north; they are uninhabited and all but trackless. Attempting travel in the mountains is more foolish even than braving my people. The only thing that makes sense is to follow the course of the Snowsblood from the plains to its source in the mountains. On foot, it should take us what — a week? ten days? — to cross shapeshifters' territory, then, if we're lucky, another ten days or two weeks to reach the source of the river."

"It doesn't sound easy," Vihena said doubtfully.

Ychass shrugged but did not reply aloud.

Karivet looked around at the group. "Perhaps we should turn back. You have braved dangers on our behalf already. It is not fair that we should ask you for anything more."

"Karivet," Remarr said quietly, "none of us has suggested turning back. Your cause is just, and we accompany you of our own free will. You need not feel responsible for us."

The others, even Ychass, nodded. For a long moment they were all silent, then Vihena spoke. "Let's go back to our camp, get some rest. Things will look better in the morning."

 *"No! No!" The stillness of the cottage was shattered by Eikoheh's cry. In the sleeping loft, Ohmiden sat bolt upright. She cried out again. He leapt up, not even bothering to straighten his nightshirt, and flung himself down the loft ladder. Despite Eikoheh's cries, he could hear the heavy thump of the treadles.*

The weaver was seated at her loom, her face contorted with anguish. Tears and sweat gleamed on her cheeks in the lamplight, while the shuttle flew through the warp. Ohmiden gripped her shoulders. "What? What is it? Can't you stop?"

She shook her head. "Look at the pattern. I've lost it."

He looked at the work on the loom. The pattern, full of gentle colors — soft browns and golds, a deep blue, a quiet green — was now interrupted by a band of vivid purple. It was the strangest thing: the thread on the shuttle in Eikoheh's hand was silver-gray, but when it touched the warp, it became deep purple. He felt a shiver of apprehension as he watched the cloth grow on the loom.

"Get me another color," Eikoheh gasped.

182

He complied, handing her a shuttle wound with the soft gold he saw elsewhere in the weaving. Eikoheh struggled with the two shuttles for a long moment, as if each had a will of its own. Finally she managed to stop the purple band from growing. She wove a thin stripe of sandy gold into the cloth before she set the shuttle down with a heavy sigh. Ohmiden rubbed her shoulders but did not speak.

"I have regained control," the weaver said after a moment, "but I fear the damage is done. They were so close — so close, Ohmiden! Success was within their grasp, when something interfered. I've never felt anything like it, anything so strong — or so malevolent." She shuddered.

"Come away," he said. "Come rest. It's late."

She nodded, rising stiffly from the loom. "Gods, I wish I'd never begun! But now I've no choice but to finish it. Tell me, Ohmiden, do you dream good news?"

He managed to hide his dismay. "My sleep has been quiet. Perhaps tonight . . ."

She looked at him sharply, as though she guessed he was lying to her. Then she shrugged. "Doubtless things will look less desperate by daylight." She stifled a yawn. "Goodnight, Dreamer."

"Goodnight, Dreamweaver."

Khehaddi's band reined in at the spring. Her lieutenant, Edevvi, looked back at her. "Do we make camp here, Captain, or ride on?"

"Make camp," she responded, swinging down from her

horse's back. "We can't reach the next spring before day-light, and I'd rather not be exposed to every eye in the dry lands, come dawn. Besides, the next water hole is a large one. The clan we've been following is almost certain to be camped there." She sighed. "The outlanders *must* be with them, if they are still alive at all. I can't understand it."

Edevvi dismounted, then loosened the girth of her saddle, a thoughtful look on her face. "If they *are* with the clan, what will we do? We can't hope to defeat an entire clan — there are only ten of us, after all."

Khehaddi looked grim. "If they're with the clan, and not prisoners, we've lost. There's no way we can stop them from reaching Windsmeet. We can only trust in the fickleness of the gods." She sighed heavily, looking about at her patrol. None of their faces reflected the weariness she felt. She wondered whether she was getting old or the stress of act-ing against her conscience was telling on her. She surprised concern on several faces and managed a reassuring smile. "No matter — we can worry over this in the morning. For now, let's get the tents up. I'm tired."

SEVENTEEN

The clan accompanied the wayfarers as far as the standing stones that marked the boundary between the desert and the shapeshifters' territory. They reached the standing stones near midnight on the second night. Emirri bade them farewell.

"I would offer you horses," she said, "but I fear they would prove a hindrance in the mountains."

Zan suppressed her surprise. By now she knew how highly the Wild Khedathi regarded their animals. "We appreciate all that you have given us, Emirri of clan Khesst, and we know there is no way to repay your kindness and generosity. We are grateful."

The clan leader shrugged. "It was kin duty; it deserves no thanks." She turned to Vihena. "Walk in peace, foster daughter. Remember, you have a place with us, Vihena, when you are done questing."

"I will remember," Vihena promised with a tight voice

as they clasped forearms in the Khedathi manner. "Walk in peace, foster mother."

The clan leader turned to Iobeh. "Shokhath asked me to tell you that by the time you have returned from the mountains, foaling season will have come and gone. He wishes you to have one of the new foals. Do not forget."

Iobeh found the horsemaster's face in the crowd of clanspeople and made the gesture for thanks in the Khedathi hand-language.

The clan leader gave a beautifully carved bone-handled throwing dagger to Karivet. "Traditionally, the gift of a weapon is accompanied by the fervent hope that it will always find its way into the hearts of one's enemies. In this case" — she smiled gently, an incongruous expression on her hard face — "I find myself hoping you will never have cause or need to use it."

He bowed slightly. "I thank you, Emirri, for the gift, for the good wishes, and for all your hospitality to us."

To the shapeshifter, Emirri gave an embroidered sash. Ychass accepted it with no outward show of emotion and a polite, colorless thanks. Zan heard her cynical thought: *Rules of hospitality can be so awkward.*

As the clan leader turned to Zan, she said, "Stranger, there is only one thing I can give you that will mean anything to you." Then she faced Remarr and bowed slightly. "Walk with the gods, Remarr."

The minstrel's eyes widened with shock, then he made his face blank. He returned her slight, formal bow. "May the gods guard you and yours, Emirri of Khesst."

Without another word, Emirri turned and walked away, taking the clan with her. Zan realized she had been holding her breath and exhaled. She caught sight of Remarr's tight face and clutched his arm. "I didn't ask her to do that."

He forced a smile. "If you had, she would have refused. She can be very difficult. But what now?" He turned to Ychass. "Do we camp here, or press on?"

She considered. "I think we had better press on. It would be best if we could reach the river before dawn. I doubt there is much cover even there, but it will be cooler. And there's no reason to camp now, since it makes most sense to continue traveling at night, at least until we leave the plains."

Without further discussion, they went on. A little before dawn they reached the river. The Snowsblood was nothing like Zan had imagined; its name made it sound clear, cold, and sparkling. In reality, it was a rather sluggish trickle of brown water in the center of a wide expanse of reeds and mud. On either side of the river, for a short distance, grew rather parched-looking grasses and some stunted bushes. When Zan started searching for a place to pitch the tent, Ychass spoke up.

"We will be less conspicuous if we forgo the tent."

There was no argument. They all found places in the dubious shelter of the bushes and bedded down. Within minutes, all were asleep.

'Tsan! The shapeshifter's thought woke her. *Don't move. Gods curse me for a thrice-damned fool — we should have set a watch.*

What is it? Zan queried.

Khedathi, from the City. They're on horseback. Can't you hear them?

Zan opened her mind. She ignored the sleeping thoughts of her companions and concentrated on casting her mind further. Yes, she heard wisps of thoughts — mounted warriors' thoughts. Carefully she edged herself up on her elbows so she could see through the scraggly branches. She noticed Iobeh's open eyes and signed carefully: *Pursuit. Warn the others.* Iobeh passed the message to Karivet and Vihena, while Zan laid a finger across Remarr's lips to wake him and warn him simultaneously. The riders were heading for the river a little to the south of their makeshift camp. They could hear the squelching of the horses' hooves in the mud; it seemed nearly as loud as their heartbeats.

Lie still, the shapeshifter thought. Zan translated this into hand-language for the others. *Curse these white robes. I should have foreseen this . . .*

What can we do? Zan thought back.

Ychass didn't shrug, but Zan could hear the resignation in her thoughts. *You tell me, Stranger.*

Zan bit her lips together. The Tame Khedathi dismounted to water their horses and fill their skins. They stood about for several minutes, apparently discussing something, though the watchers in the bushes could not hear any voices. Zan caught wisps of thought about whether to press on or to camp. *They're thinking about camping here,* she signed to the others.

For an age, they watched the warriors. Gradually Zan's thudding heart slowed. She began to notice the gentle, soothing hum of insects; the sun was warm and lulling. Muzzily she looked around. The others were similarly soothed, except Iobeh, whose face was intent, eyes narrowed in concentration. Understanding came to Zan, and she silently warned Ychass not to interfere. The shapeshifter forced her drooping eyes open and nodded slightly. Minutes passed, many minutes. Finally Ychass touched Zan's mind. *The pursuers are all asleep. We'd better move. How long will the sleep last?*

Zan shrugged, gently waking the others. She touched Iobeh's shoulder last. The girl blinked and looked up at her. *Let's go,* Zan signed, *before they wake.*

They gathered their gear as stealthily as they could, then rose and started upriver. Ychass led them to a grassy path that ran close to the muddy bed of the river. The footing was even and the grass muffled their steps. *We should run,* Ychass suggested. *No point in wasting this miracle.*

Zan signed to the others and they all set out at an easy lope, trying to cover as much ground as possible before their pursuers awoke. They ran until their sides ached and their breath wheezed in their throats. When they could run no longer, they walked until their breathing slowed, then ran again. They kept up the pace until the sun was sliding toward the horizon and their legs felt as if they would fall off.

But what good has it done us? Vihena signed when they halted. *They are mounted.*

We're still free, Karivet pointed out. *Maybe they'll lose our trail.*

Trail! Ychass thought, for the first time with something

like real hope. *We have to go a little farther, 'Tsan. Tell the others.*

Swallowing a sigh, Zan relayed the information to the others. They suppressed groans, but followed when Ychass led them into the water. *We're breaking our trail,* she thought; Zan signed for the others. *Follow the river for at least another mile, maybe two, while I try to really confuse them.*

They set off up the shallow river, while Ychass waded across and began laying a false trail. When Zan looked back over her shoulder, she was surprised to see Ychass in the shape of a small Oratheh, leaving a careful set of footprints from the muddy riverbed through the brush to the stony land beyond, where she shifted to a bird and flew back to the river. She repeated the process in the shapes of the others before rejoining them.

They waded until they came to a place where the muddy riverbed was interrupted by a jumble of large stones, then they climbed out of the water, careful to leave only wet tracks on the stones. Ychass herded them all away from the riverbank into another scraggly stand of bushes, where they wearily made camp. They were all too tired to talk, and too nervous. They made a meager meal of journey bread and strips of dried meat the Khesst had given them, then they settled back to sleep for the night. Even though Zan was not sure she could keep her eyes open, she agreed to take the first watch. Ychass would take the second, waking them well before moonset so that they could get a few hours of travel in before the sun came up.

As Zan settled herself as comfortably as she could for the night's watching, she became aware of another's presence. For a heartbeat she froze, then she realized it was Remarr. She could barely make out his features in the darkness.

"What is it?" she asked him in a whisper.

"I thought you couldn't work enchantments," he whispered back accusingly.

"I can't—I didn't. It was Iobeh. She made them feel at peace."

He was silent. It took all of Zan's resolve to keep from probing his thoughts. Suddenly they both stiffened as another person approached: Iobeh. She looked at them both with weary eyes and signed, *They had ridden hard and were very tired. It would never have worked otherwise.*

The minstrel looked from Zan to the small girl, then smiled. "It was well done, Iobeh," he whispered. "Well done indeed."

She met his eyes. *Then will you stop feeling such distress, so I can get some sleep?*

His smile was lopsided. "I'll try," he murmured. "Goodnight, 'Tsan," he added as he and Iobeh moved away. Zan smothered a sigh as she watched them go.

Far downriver from where the fugitives camped, the call of a night bird woke Captain Khehaddi. She sat up with a curse. It was fully dark; she had never meant them to sleep the day away. "Edevvi!" she shouted, anger sharpening her voice. Her lieutenant sprang to attention from where she had supposedly been standing guard.

"Captain?"

The sound of Edevvi's voice recalled the captain to where they were and the danger surrounding them. She continued in hand-language. *Fine guard, you. Didn't think you were green enough to fall asleep at your post.*

Nor did I, Captain. It won't happen again.

Indeed not. Khehaddi's expression was grim.

Now what? Do we follow them now?

The captain shook her head. *Not enough light for tracking. Set watches who won't fall asleep. We'll spend the rest of the night here.*

Edevvi nodded once, then went about her task. She was glad the night was dark enough to hide her blush.

EIGHTEEN

 Morning found the two groups of travelers moving away from one another. Ychass led her companions along the Snowsblood, into the rich golden grasslands of the plains, while the Tame Khedathi took the shapeshifter's false trail and were heading across the stony heath to the northeast of the river. Long before the sun had climbed to noon, Ychass called a halt. She showed the others how to rub earth into their white robes, to make them less noticeable, then they made a makeshift camp in the tall grasses.

"I still think we will be wisest to travel at night, as long as the footing is fairly even," Ychass explained. "We'll spend the day here, and travel once dusk falls. In the meantime, perhaps someone can catch us some fish for supper."

Karivet volunteered, and spent the next few hours crouched beside the river, trying to tickle the river dwellers into his hands. He did well, too, catching three good-sized fish. As he cleaned them with his new knife, Ychass started a small fire. She took care with the fuel so there would be little smoke. Karivet watched her preparations until, very pleased with himself, he settled down for a nap.

The day passed quietly. Late in the afternoon, they gathered for a meal of fish stew and journey bread, then stored their gear and set out.

The walking was harder than in the desert. The grass hid the occasional unevenness of the ground, and sometimes the stems tangled up around their feet, trying to trip them. No one actually fell, though, and despite their stumbling, they made reasonably good time. At sunrise they halted.

Days passed uneventfully, and they began to be lulled by the emptiness of the plains. They didn't quite grow careless, but they began to forget why they were being careful. It was clear they had eluded their Khedathi pursuers — Ychass told them that the stony heath stretched for several days' journey before it came to an end near one of the most populated stretches of shapeshifter territory. It was likely the Khedathi would have their hands too full of their own fates to worry about the motley company, no matter how desperately the travelers were wanted in the City.

In all this time, the group's biggest worry was food. Their supplies, though they had been augmented by the Khesst, would not last forever. Since the plains were less harsh than the dry lands, Ychass suggested they try to live off the land. Everyone helped. Karivet and Iobeh caught fish in the river, and Remarr often snared rabbits. Ychass showed them some tubers and a type of reed that stewed up well, and Zan and Vihena grew adept at gathering them.

194

As the days passed, they began to leave the plains behind them. Now, as the river climbed, they saw occasional trees, the edible reeds became scarce, and the days were cooler.

Their night travel became treacherous; they could only travel when there was enough moonlight to see by, since a false step could have disastrous consequences. They developed a new pattern, starting out before sunset and going until it was fully dark, then resting until moonrise and traveling until moonset; if they could, they traveled a little farther in the cold gray hour before sunrise. This slowed them down, and Ychass chafed at the delay. The only comfort they could hold out to her was that they were able to avoid eating any of their dried supplies, since they had more waking time during the day to seek food.

Near moonset one night, when they were all tired from an arduous stretch of climbing, they reached a place that sent shivers up and down Zan's spine. Off to their right the river hissed and frothed at the bottom of a deep, narrow gorge. The landscape around them was strewn with huge boulders that loomed half buried, like ruined statues. The waning moon played hide-and-seek with scudding clouds, making the boulders' shadows seem particularly deep and mysterious. Zan, walking beside Ychass, hesitated and put out one hand to stop the shapeshifter. Ychass looked at her in the dark, a question in her mind. Vihena joined them, her blade whispering out of its sheath.

"What's wrong?" she breathed.

Zan shrugged her shoulders.

"Uncanny place," Vihena agreed. "Shall I go first?"

Zan forced a smile. "No, I'm just letting my nerves get the better of me. I didn't mean to alarm you."

Vihena stepped back a pace and Ychass met Zan's eyes. *Just nerves?*

I don't know, Zan admitted. *Do you feel it?*

Ychass shook her head. Zan stepped into the shadow of the first boulder. A faint sound made her look up. She froze, battling panic. She was practically nose to nose with a large feline. It had human eyes. Deep in its throat, a growl began.

What do you want? Zan thought at it fiercely.

Its head jerked back in surprise. Then it growled more loudly. Several other big cats slunk out of the shadows, blocking her path.

We want the renegade, the cat responded, *and perhaps your lives as well. You trespass.*

We mean you no harm, Zan thought. *We are merely passing through your lands on a quest for the gods.*

The shapeshifter's thoughts quivered with unpleasant laughter. *Indeed. Then undoubtedly your divine patron will stop us from doing as we will. The renegade is ours.*

The other shapeshifters knit their thoughts with those of the first. It was an unpleasant sensation, the feeling that their minds were joined into a suffocating whole colored with ugly anticipation, through which Zan's and Ychass's mental voices could not pierce. The cats turned toward Ychass menacingly. *You are nameless, renegade — Outcast, rejected, rebuffed.* Their thought-voices battered like a strong wind. *We denounce you; we deny you; you have no place with us. We make you unchanging, unnamed, unliving.*

196

We take your name; we bid your shape; we destroy your being. You are kinless, spiritless, nameless.

Zan saw Ychass's desperate eyes. She grabbed her arm and shook it. *You're not nameless,* she thought fiercely. *You're Ychass. They can't do this to you!*

We bid your shape, they repeated. Their united thoughts swamped Zan's mind with malice. She wanted to slam mental gates against them, but she couldn't leave Ychass to face them alone. *Hound,* they went on inexorably. *Hound to grovel and cringe. You who were too proud to obey us will be forced to lick the heels of the City folk.*

Under her hand Zan could feel Ychass's form begin to dissolve. *No!* she flung at them, desperation ringing shrilly in her thought-voice. Her hand gripped Ychass's arm even more tightly, as though her touch could anchor Ychass in her shape. *You are not nameless! You gave me your name, Ychass: I give it back.* Her thought-voice suddenly gained authority and power. *I give you back your name! You are Ychass! YCHASS!*

The shapeshifters' united thought unraveled abruptly into confusion. Thoughts spun in Zan's mind like sparks when a fire has been kicked. *Namegiver!* one of them thought; half a title, half an accusation. Zan felt the hairs prickle on her forearms. Beside her, Ychass drew herself up.

Go! Ychass told them. *You are powerless to harm me — you cannot take my name! Go! I do not need a place with you; I will make a place of my own! I do not need your kinship; I will make ties of my own! You cannot touch my spirit; it is beyond your reach! Go hence!*

It would seem we cannot punish you as the law bids, one of the shapeshifters said, *but still you trespass.*

Zan tried to feign unconcern. *I told you: we are questing for the gods.*

They changed shape so quickly it was dizzying. For a moment five huge falcons hung on the air. *I doubt that will matter to the Temple, but we will tell them. We go. We will return.* In a flurry of wings, they departed.

"Well," said Vihena. "What was that all about?"

"They tried to punish me for returning here," Ychass replied. "They tried to make me a hound for the tribute. They failed, and they fled."

"Why didn't they attack us?" Remarr asked. "There were five of them and only six of us. Surely the odds weren't *that* long."

"'Tsan upset them. She hears thoughts. They were unprepared for that."

The others seemed satisfied, but Zan thought uneasily, *There was more to it than that, wasn't there? I wish I understood all that name business.*

Still playing innocent? Ychass retorted, cynicism bitter in her thoughts. *Don't you think you're overdoing it?*

I don't understand, Ychass.

Then you have infallible instincts, 'Tsan. But I'm being ungrateful. Once again I must thank you for my freedom. I gave you my name, but I must admit I never expected you to give it back. I suppose it's overly cynical of me to wonder what else you want from me?

"I don't want anything from you," Zan said softly. "Can't you believe that?"

The shapeshifter shrugged her thin shoulders, but her smile was calculating, and her thoughts said no.

Khehaddi had not spent a restful night. She had found it impossible to sleep with one hand chained to the wall and her mind full of questions and worries. She had been separated from the members of her patrol, and she did not have any way of knowing how they were faring. And she kept tormenting herself by wondering whether she had done the right thing when she ordered them to put away their weapons and go peacefully with the shapeshifters. She had gambled all their lives on the chance that the shapeshifters would be reasonable — and none of the tales her people told encouraged her to think it a wise risk. But they had been outnumbered, and truly in the wrong, and she could think of no other action that promised even a slim chance. It had been a long, doubt-filled night, and it was with a feeling akin to relief that she heard footsteps coming toward her cell. One way or the other, the waiting would soon be over.

It was not the guard Khehaddi had expected. Instead, a woman in a plain, undyed caftan put the key to the lock and stepped inside. She was strange to Khehaddi's eyes; her long hair was light brown, her skin was not as fair as a Vematheh's but rather sallow, and her eyes were peculiar, a gray so pale it was almost colorless. She regarded Khehaddi impassively. When she spoke, her voice had a curious sibilant accent, and her words came slowly, as though she were unused to speech.

"So you are the fool who thought to invade our lands with a troop of ten."

"We are not invaders, Lady. We seek fugitives. Their trail led us into your land."

"Fugitives from City justice who survived the dry lands? At least tell a believable lie, Khedatheh."

Khehaddi clenched both fists and fought her temper. This woman did not know it was a death insult to accuse a Khedath of lying; it was not her fault. She exhaled slowly. "I do not tell lies, Lady, good or bad. There was someone from the desert to guide them in the dry lands."

"So. Who are they whom you seek?"

Khehaddi shrugged. "There are six of them. Two children from the forest, a man from the desert, a woman from the City, a stranger, and one of your people."

For the first time an emotion registered on the shapeshifter's face: surprise. "Of *my* people? Who?"

"I do not know her name," Khehaddi replied. "She was a slave in a City merchant's house."

The woman's breath hissed between her teeth. "So. That one. It is death for her to come here. She knows that, and she is no fool. Why do you believe they came into our lands?"

Khehaddi turned her free hand palm upward. "We followed their tracks. They led across the river and into the stony heath."

The woman was silent. Khehaddi watched her anxiously, but could read nothing in her impassive face.

"Lady, I will make you a promise," Khehaddi said when she could bear the silence no longer. "If you free me and the others of my patrol, we will not rest until they have been taken."

"No," she replied immediately. "We will find them and deal with them ourselves. I will send you and your people back to the dry lands with a warning and a promise. Once we have been lenient and overlooked your trespass. A second time we will rend you all limb from limb, with no questions and no quarter. Do you understand? Will you promise to leave our lands and not return?"

Khehaddi nodded. "I understand. I give you my word we will not return, and I thank you for your graciousness, Lady."

The shapeshifter nodded. "I trust I will not later have cause to regret my leniency." There was threat in the long look she gave Khehaddi. Then she went away without looking back. A few minutes later, the guards came to open Khehaddi's shackle.

NINETEEN

Ohmiden woke with a start, his heart thudding painfully. He was not sure whether he had cried out. The dream had been vivid and terrifying, and what it said of the danger of the twins and their companions he didn't want to consider. If the gods were merciful, Eikoheh would be sleeping, unsuspecting. He eased himself up onto one elbow to see. The weaver's face was level with his own as she stood on the ladder to the loft. She raised an eyebrow.

"I made some tea when you began to dream," she said. "Why don't you come have some while you tell me about it?"

He hardly sighed. Much as he wanted to spare the weaver, he knew she was tougher than he liked to think—and shrewder. He would have to tell her all of it; she would resent any prevarication.

Eikoheh studied him over the rim of her mug. "Well?" she asked at last.

"It's not good," he said heavily. "My dreams are full of

people wearing beasts' faces. I fear our friends have strayed into the country of the shapeshifters. I dreamed of a servant of the gods, a woman, who holds much power over them. She has two faces, neither of them kind." He fell silent.

"Two faces?" Eikoheh prompted. "What are they? Animal faces?"

"No," Ohmiden replied, remembering. "She wears a mask and carries another. They are rage and fear. The answer to either is often death."

Eikoheh was silent, pondering. Finally she nodded. "Then I will weave fear for her, deep fear. I will weave her a fear so full of awe that she will not dare to harm them."

The weaver's voice was so strong and certain that Ohmiden looked at her in surprise. "Will that work?" he asked.

The certainty evaporated as Eikoheh hunched a shoulder. "We can only hope."

"So," Edevvi said to her captain as they drew rein on the wide heath, "we go home? We leave the Utverassi to deal with our quarry?"

Khehaddi studied her lieutenant, seeing the unease lying behind her words, and shook her head. "I dare not. After all, there is a shapeshifter with them. I know she is Outcast, but so was the minstrel. They might somehow convince the Utverassi to leave them alone."

"But you can't mean to take us back into Utverassi lands," one of the others protested. "You told them —"

"I gave my word." Khehaddi cut him off. Though she smiled, there was bitterness in her tone. "That still has some value. No, we will not pursue the fugitives any farther. Rather, I think we should wait for them. My guess is that the gods have set them a task to perform. If I'm right, they will have to return to Windsmeet. I suggest we make camp at that small spring we passed — the one nearest the hill. When they return, if they do, we will be ready for them."

"How long will we wait, Captain?" another asked.

She shrugged. "That is not a decision I can make on my own. Tholenn, Fenorreh, once we're out of Utverassi lands, I want you to return to the City and report to Belerann and the Lord. Explain the situation and return with orders. Is that clear?"

The two she had singled out nodded.

"For the rest of us," she added, "this means at least another two weeks, or three, in the dry lands. I trust no one is desperately homesick."

For the next few days, the companions traveled during the day. They reasoned that since the shapeshifters knew they were there, they might as well abandon secrecy and take advantage of the sunlight. It wasn't reasonable, Zan reflected, but traveling by day lifted her spirits, and she often found herself humming to herself in the crisp, bright mornings.

The terrain had changed again. They traveled in a wide valley carved by the river, through scattered copses of beech, ash, and birch. In the stretches of meadow they could see the mountains ahead of them: towering peaks brushed with white leaning against the clear sky. They were beautiful, but formidable. Every time Zan caught sight of them, she felt a clench of awe.

The twins enjoyed this leg of the journey; they skipped and danced among the trees, whistling birdcalls to one another in their pleasure to be in places that reminded them of home. Vihena often joined them, learning from them the calls of birds she had never seen. In the evenings Remarr played his harp and sang, and told tales that set them all to laughing — all except Ychass. The shapeshifter had always been aloof, but now she almost never spoke. She watched them with an impassive face, but her thoughts were full of the tag-ends of old worries. Even Zan couldn't draw her out. Mention of the Temple had deeply troubled the shapeshifter, Zan gathered, but she was unable to cajole any further information.

One evening, after a supper of fish and rabbit, they sat about the fire while Remarr drew quiet music from his harp. The wind was off the mountains and chilly, so they huddled in their robes and sat as near to the fire as they could. Suddenly Ychass raised her head like a deer scenting danger. She demanded silence with a hand.

"We have visitors," she whispered.

A moment later a small flock of birds dropped out of the air and became people at the edges of the ring of their camp. One woman, dressed in a simple caftan of undyed material, stepped forward. "You trespass," she said with deliberation, "and you shelter one who has been cast out. The penalty for either offense is death."

Ychass rose to her feet, pushing her hood back so that the woman could see her face. "Priestess, the fault is mine. I knew the penalties, but did not keep the laws."

That has ever been your way, the priestess thought. *Have you not learned better yet?*

It would seem not, Ychass returned. "Priestess, do not punish these others for my failings. I will submit myself to your justice if you will permit the others to pass."

Zan sprang up angrily. "No! I will not accept freedom at such a cost." She turned to the priestess. "We have caused your people no harm, and we intend none. If indeed you have a law forbidding trespass, perhaps you also have the wisdom to set it aside when it is unnecessary."

"I have your word that you are harmless," the priestess retorted, "but of what value are words? My people are few; you, the unchanging, are many. You fear us, hate us — how can I ever accept that your people mean my people no harm? To what judgment would the gods call me if I let you spy out the secrets of our lands and live?"

"Secrets?" Zan demanded, exasperated. "We haven't even been to the far side of the Snowsblood; we've seen neither town nor dwelling place. What secrets do you hide among the stones and river water that are worth lives to keep?"

"As priestess in the Temple, I am the keeper of the laws the gods gave us. You have broken them. The penalties are clear."

Zan ran a hand distractedly through her hair, pushing back her hood. "But there are exceptions to every law. Haven't your gods told you that?" Her anger had begun to pale to despair; she wasn't getting through. She dropped her hand with a sigh. "What can I say to convince you?"

The priestess was staring at her, her nostrils flared. *"Who are you?"* the priestess demanded, her voice tight.

Zan's stomach clenched suddenly. She didn't understand this — something was going on, something critically important, and she had no idea what. The priestess's tightly closed mind gave her no clues. Zan chose her words with care, managing to keep her voice cool and her uncertainty out of the forefront of her mind. "One of your people called me Namegiver. That will do."

No! The priestess's mental denial was ripped out of her, then quickly stifled. "You mock me," she said through stiff lips.

"Indeed, I do not," Zan replied. The reaction wasn't anger; it was fear. She tried to put the discussion back on track. "I am merely asking whether the gods did not tell you that there are exceptions to every law."

The priestess laughed suddenly, harshly. "Clearly there are, so make your exception — and abide by it."

Zan drew breath. She wasn't sure she trusted this capitulation. Was it a trap? She'd have to risk it. "With your gracious permission, we will continue our quest. We will not stray more than a mile from the river until such time as we are ready to return to the dry lands."

The priestess smiled thinly. "So it is only an exception for you? We aren't to give up our lives and lands to some new, favored people?" Her sarcasm grew more pronounced. "We aren't to step aside for the unchanging ones? We aren't to be pushed down while you raise up someone else? How tolerant you are — or do we amuse you? Surely it isn't mercy that bids you spare us."

Zan frowned. She didn't understand. She had no power over the shapeshifters; what did the priestess mean, "spare us"? But she had to say something. "Lady, it is not mine to decide the fate of your people, but . . . but I think a world without you who change would be much the poorer," she said softly.

A glint of triumph shone in the priestess's eyes, and her fleeting smile held malice. "The laws we follow were made to safeguard us. You say you would mourn our passing, but you break our laws. You make your allowed exception; one law we have set aside for you. But that is not all you ask. You travel with one who, according to the gods' laws, is Outcast. She is dead to us because she has ignored the laws that guard the safety of our people. We could permit her to live only as long as she was bound in a shape, among foreigners. There is no repeal, especially not now, after she has shared her mind with strangers. She is worse than dead to us — she is an affront, living evidence of contempt for our people, the people you claim to value, and our laws. And you travel with her!"

Zan put her arm around Ychass's shoulders, meeting her eyes briefly. "She did not share her mind with strangers, she shared her mind with *me*. But do you not think she has paid penalty enough for her offenses? To be cast, aware and helpless, among foreigners who fear and despise one is no easy fate."

"It was not meant to be an easy fate. It was meant to be her death," the priestess said coldly.

Zan released Ychass and spread her hands. "And so it was. The renegade you feared is gone — what haughty spirit could survive the punishment you set? But I have shared minds with the woman who stands here, and she with me, and that has changed us both. You cast her out, and you were right to do so. But I have taken her in, which was also right — and I am glad of it."

The priestess did not reply while the silence grew taut. Finally she bowed, an elaborate, graceful, ceremonial gesture. As she rose, she held Zan's gaze for a moment, searchingly. "I have always thought my masters merciless; you make me doubt. Go in peace, but do not stray from the river." She gestured to her company, and the shapeshifters took to the air and wheeled away.

Zan watched them dwindle to specks against the dimming sky. After a moment she turned to Ychass with a question, but the words stuck in her throat. Ychass was weeping; silent tears ran down her cheeks. As Zan watched, Ychass caught a tear on one finger and stared at it, then she closed her hand abruptly and shifted shape. Before Zan could react, the wolf was racing off upstream.

"Ychass!" she cried. "*Ychass!*" But the shapeshifter did not respond. Zan began to take off after her, but Remarr caught her shoulder.

"Wait," he said quietly. "You can't hope to overtake her. She'll come back."

"But —"

He shook his head, silencing her. "I can't claim to understand everything that passed, 'Tsan, but I think she may need to be alone. According to legend, the shapeshifters are incapable of tears."

With an inarticulate protest, Zan sat down beside the fire and covered her face with her hands. She sat that way for a long time while Remarr played quietly and the others did the dishes in the river. Finally she raised her head. Her eyes met the minstrel's briefly, then she dropped her gaze to the shifting dance of the flames.

"I wish I understood," she murmured into the whisper of the fire and the quiet harp. "They think I do — the priestess, Ychass. But I don't. I feel I'm in a maze made of mirrors: I can't tell where the walls are, much less the openings, and when I look down, all I see is reflections stretching off to infinity. I can't even tell whether I'm standing on reality or illusion, or if I've already begun to fall."

Remarr was silent; his music changed. Zan recognized the round she had taught him, "Dona Nobis Pacem." As the familiar phrases unfolded, her throat tightened. She bowed her head and finally let herself cry, and with her silent tears came peace.

TWENTY

By the time they rose the next morning, Ychass had returned. The shapeshifter behaved as if nothing had happened, and the others followed her lead. They made good time that day and the next; by the third, they were in the mountains. Their travel slowed. Gone were the easy rises and gently rolling meadows. Over the centuries, spring floodwaters of the Snowsblood had carved a deep defile in the granite of the mountains. This late in the season, enough of the flood had abated to expose the jumbled rocks by the sides. Though the route was steep and treacherous, they made their way over these rocks, for the banks were too overgrown to allow passage. With frequent stops to rest, the little company made its careful progress over stones slick with spray and moss. As they climbed, suitable places to camp became scarce. Their first night, they camped on a ledge of rock barely wide enough for all of them to stretch out; the next night, they

were lucky to discover a small, dank cave behind a waterfall. That night they had no fire, for the only wood they could find was too wet to burn cleanly and the little cave would have been unbearable full of smoke. No one slept well; the damp ate away at their comfort. By morning they were stiff and cramped. To make matters worse, it was raining.

"I never thought I'd *complain* about water falling from the sky," Remarr remarked sourly as they set out into the steady drizzle.

"Isn't it amazing how traveling broadens one's outlook?" Zan asked with sarcastic cheer. "No doubt we should all be grateful."

"I'd be a good deal more grateful if I'd had a hot breakfast," Karivet put in.

"Don't talk about heat," Vihena said with a groan. "I'll never be warm again. My poor feet are numb, and that doesn't help matters, ei —" She broke off with a sharp gasp as her foot slipped. Zan turned in time to see her hands frantically scrabbling as she slid toward the lip of the river.

Ychass reacted fastest. Before the others moved or cried out, she took the shape of a large mountain eagle. Beating her wings strongly, she sunk her talons into the leather of Vihena's pack and supported her until she could get her legs under her again and crawl to safety.

No one said anything while Vihena caught her breath and Ychass again took human shape. Finally Vihena managed a weak smile for the others. "That will teach me to complain. I'd have been a good deal colder if I'd landed in the river." She turned to the shapeshifter. "Thank you, Ychass."

Ychass regarded her gravely. "You are welcome, Vihena," she replied.

Suddenly Zan's eyes widened. *My God, I forgot — I spoke your name aloud. Oh, Ychass, I'm sorry!*

Ychass turned her strange colorless eyes on Zan. *It doesn't matter, Stranger. You gave my name back to me. It has lost its power to bind me.*

I don't understand, Zan thought, feeling suddenly as though she couldn't help but repeat this weary refrain over and over.

To her surprise, Ychass responded. *When the gods made the world, they called life out of nothingness by naming it. The shapeshifters remember this. When children reach the threshold of adulthood, the Temple names them, binding them to the people. The name the Temple uses for an individual is not given, it is lent, and the Temple may reclaim it — and the person's life and freedom with it. The name Ychass is mine, not the Temple's; no one can bind me with it unless I give them that power. Namegiver, you made me free.*

Zan shivered. Ychass's thoughts touched her in uncomfortable places. *But why do the shapeshifters put up with it? Surely they don't all want the Temple to have so much power over them?*

Ychass's mental laughter was bitter with self-mockery. *You and I are too much alike. It was that sort of thinking that got me exiled in the first place.*

Zan almost held her breath, hoping Ychass would tell her more and afraid to disturb her in any way.

I didn't think the Temple should be all-powerful, she went on a little ruefully. *The priestess whom you outfaced so brilliantly had determined that I should serve the gods in their House. It was an honor, but not one I cared for. I told her so, and it angered her. She threatened me with the tribute, and I was afraid, so I asked my sister to trade names with me, so that the Temple would have no power over either of us. I was not sure it would work — to this day I do not know, for she betrayed me. I was punished, and when I still refused to serve the gods in their House, I was cast out and banished.*

Why did you still refuse even after you were punished, when you knew what the dangers were? Zan asked gently.

Ychass's thought-voice was full of conviction and power. *Because it was wrong. The gods deserve better than to be served out of fear. I could not do justice to the task demanded of me.*

Zan was silent for several moments, awed by Ychass's revelation. Finally she thought, *It was brave of you, Ychass. Surely the gods appreciate that.*

Ychass met her eyes, her own expression enigmatic. *Surely they must.*

After Vihena's near disaster they climbed even more carefully, and there were no other close calls. As the afternoon wore toward evening, they began to look for a place to camp, but they saw nothing even remotely suitable. Wearily they pressed on, but as the light got worse, they began to discuss their problem.

"I don't much fancy perching on a rock for the night," Vihena said, "but I don't know what else to suggest. With the rain, there won't even be a moon, and it would be fatally stupid to blunder around in the dark."

"But there's hardly even anything to perch on," Zan protested. "In this situation, *falling* asleep takes on a whole new, nasty meaning. I think we should press on and hope for the best. I know it's getting murky, but it's not impossible yet."

"We haven't passed anyplace we could stop for the past three hours. What makes you think the next ten minutes will make any difference?" Remarr asked. "We have rope. Perhaps we can anchor ourselves, so that if we nod off we won't fall."

"Great. We can be hung in our sleep," Zan snapped.

Oh, please! Iobeh signed. *I'm too tired for a fight.*

"Look," Karivet broke in, pointing. "Light."

They followed his gesture. Ahead of them they could see a flicker of yellow light. They all gazed at it for several moments before Vihena spoke.

"It's not the right color for firelight. If we were in civilized parts, I'd say it was lamplight, but who would live up here?"

It's the god's House, Iobeh signed. *It must be! Let's go. Maybe we can reach it before dark.*

Ychass spoke up. "Distances are deceptive in the mountains. It could be a mile or more away — too far to reach tonight."

"But to be so close . . ." Zan protested.

"Being close won't do us a bit of good if our broken bodies are at the bottom of the gorge," Vihena said.

While the others argued, Karivet and Remarr knotted ropes into harnesses around their chests and arms. Without discussion, Ychass took the ends of the ropes, shifted to bird shape, and flew up into the overhanging trees. After a moment she dropped the ends down to be secured; they were looped over sturdy tree limbs. With a sigh, Zan copied Remarr and Karivet. When they were all harnessed, they settled back to wait out the night. In the drizzle, it was thoroughly uncomfortable. They were all glad when the pale dawn offered enough light to move on.

After two hours of travel, they were beginning to wonder whether they had imagined the light the night before. As the river climbed farther into the mountains, its course became even steeper. At the crest of one taxing stretch, they were confronted by a sheer cliff. The river spilled in a silver column from the top of a wall of gray granite. The cliff was so sharply undercut that the wall of stone appeared to be leaning toward them. They stared at it in dismay. Suddenly Iobeh pointed.

There are windows in the cliff, she signed.

Sure enough, near the top of the cliff were patches of a darker gray in the shape of narrow arched windows.

"Well," Zan remarked, "I wonder where the doorway is."

While she was speaking, Karivet moved forward. Carefully skirting the pool into which the waterfall pounded, he vanished behind it. A moment later he reappeared, signing, *There are steps cut into the cliff.*

216

The others made their way to him. The steps were old and worn, slimed with moss and very steep. At one time there had been a heavy chain strung to serve as a railing, but time and dampness had eaten it to a rusted remnant. Zan looked up and shivered. They had a long way to climb.

Since the noise of the water made conversation impossible, she signed to the others: *I think we'd better go one at a time. I'll start.* Before anyone could object, she started up the narrow stairway. Once she got going, it wasn't so bad — as long as she didn't look back. She used both her hands and her feet, since the steps were rough enough to offer good holds for her hands.

As Zan neared the top of the cliff she passed a rough stone arch, from which the waterfall issued. The stairway continued upward to a flat, grassy summit. She settled herself in the sunlight and touched thoughts with Ychass to tell her to send the next person up. She closed her eyes and tilted her face toward the sun, enjoying the warm, humming quiet.

Quite suddenly she realized she was no longer alone. She turned her head and found herself staring up into the face of a stranger. He was tall and thin, clothed in a muted silvery gray that made the vivid russet of his hair all the more startling. His face expressed friendly curiosity as he studied her, but there was something disturbing about him. Despite his red hair and unwrinkled skin, his eyes seemed ancient, and gave his face an ageless quality. Beside him sat a fox cub, who watched Zan with expectant eyes. With an effort, Zan found her tongue.

"You must be the god we were sent to find," she said.

" 'We'? I see only one of you." His voice was light, with an undertone of laughter — not the voice of a god as Zan had imagined it. The amusement in his eyes deepened.

"The others are coming," she told him. "We thought it would be better if only one climbed at a time."

"Who sent you?" he asked.

"The god we met at Windsmeet," she told him. "She sent us here on a quest."

His eyebrows rose, then he nodded. "Now I see."

"I wish I did," Zan muttered.

In one fluid motion, the god sat down beside her. The fox came over and pushed its cold nose into her hand. "What would you understand that you do not?"

"Everything," she replied feelingly.

He cocked his head to one side and looked at her quizzically. "Wouldn't you find that dull? Besides, it could make you insufferable to your friends."

She scowled at him. He was laughing at her. But he looked so innocent, and the lurking twinkle was so engaging that she found herself smiling in spite of herself. "I suppose so," she admitted, "but I *do* wish I knew why the shapeshifters set aside their laws at my request."

He shrugged. "That's easy. They thought you were a god."

Zan gaped. "A *god?*" she demanded. "Why?"

"Two reasons," he replied, and he reached out a hand and gently tugged a wisp of hair that had escaped from under her hood.

"My *hair?* But . . ." Then comprehension dawned. "You mean, all the gods have red hair?"

He nodded. Though his tone was grave, he had a smile as he said, "My mother, who orders the world, has a tidy mind. Her peoples are — distinct, and easily identified."

"Color-coded," Zan said with a gasp of almost hysterical laughter. Then her eyes narrowed. "Two reasons, you said."

He nodded. "What did you tell the shapeshifters to call you?"

Zan frowned, remembering. "I said their people had called me Namegiver . . ." She trailed off, meeting his expectant eyes. "I still don't understand."

Concern knit his brows together for an instant. "My brothers and sisters and I have use-names as well as true names. I am the Weaver; there is the Harvester, the Dreamer, the Star Sower, the Namegiver —"

Zan cut him off with a small, shocked gasp. "Oh no. But I'm not one — a god, I mean."

He shrugged again. "I didn't say you were, only that the shapeshifters thought you one. I do not know what you are, yet, or what you will be. Tell me your name."

"Alexandra Scarsdale," she said, the name feeling peculiar in her mouth. "They call me 'Tsan."

"I am Elgonar; remember that. But look — that must be one of your friends."

Zan followed his gesture and saw Karivet's head at the edge of the cliff. He scrambled up the last stair and came toward them. The fox trotted forward to investigate. Karivet's eyes widened, and he bowed to the god, who smiled at him.

"If I'd realized you were coming, I'd have repaired the stairway," he told them. "I have company so seldom it hardly seems worth the effort."

"It's not so bad," Karivet replied, "if you don't look down."

When everyone had gathered at the top of the stairs, Elgonar led them along a narrow path that crossed the crest of the hill and wound in slow switchbacks down to the wide front door of his house. The house was a vast dwelling carved from the bones of the mountain. Beyond the door was a wide flight of steps leading down to a huge entrance hall. The river ran through the center of the hall, spanned by a narrow, arching bridge, and the place was full of the river's music.

Elgonar led them across the bridge and through several dim chambers to a room with great windows that looked out of the cliff. The view was stunning. The mountains stretched before them, flattening slowly to the pale plains in the distance, with the river glinting in the landscape like a silver thread in a tapestry. For a moment Zan could only gaze in wonder; then, with an effort, she turned her attention to the room. Its walls were hung with tapestries to lessen the chill, and the floor was covered with thick carpets. For all that, it was a cold room, full of the scent of damp stone. The furniture was sparse: several wooden chairs and a couple of low tables set with oil lamps. A huge loom dominated half of the chamber. Zan's eyes were drawn to the work on it; then she knit her brows and went for a closer look. It wasn't a trick of the light: the cloth on the loom was growing, though no one was working it. She looked a question at Elgonar, who smiled slightly.

"It's the Loom of Fate," he said softly. "Sometimes I get weary, so I let the pattern come from a Dreamweaver's loom. See, this is an intricate one. That gray" — he gestured — "that's my color. It isn't often a Dreamweaver attempts to weave my Fate."

Karivet and Iobeh exchanged stricken looks. "Eikoheh," he whispered. "She's weaving a Fate for us."

Elgonar nodded.

"But it's dangerous for her," Karivet protested. "She shouldn't have begun."

Elgonar touched the boy's cheek gently. "And haring off to Windsmeet is safe? We are all reckless when need calls us."

The weaving on the Loom caught Zan's attention again and she traced the patterns with her eyes. Six strands of color occurred throughout; the god's gray first appeared alone with the deep red strand. "Do we all have colors?" she asked. "That red, is it me?" At Elgonar's nod, she shook her head in bewilderment. "Is that all we are, colors in a Dreamweaver's loom? Don't we have any more reality than that? Do we merely tread out the Fate she weaves for us?"

"No." It was Ychass who spoke. "My peo — the shape-shifters say that the gods choose the colors, but we make the patterns."

Elgonar nodded. "Look." He pointed to a place in the weaving where a strange, vivid purple interrupted the pattern. "That is my sister whom you met at Windsmeet. Your Dreamweaver did not plan on her interference. The pattern shows that she was unprepared for it — she recovered, but the pattern changed. You see, the Loom merely guides, it does not govern."

"But your sister is a god," Zan pointed out. "Of course a god can change the pattern, but that doesn't mean *we* can."

Elgonar turned one hand palm upward. "What are you, Stranger, if not a break in Fate's pattern? What are any of you? I see a Vematheh with a sword and a Khedathen without one, a shapeshifter who weeps and two Orathi who have left their forest and yet live. You are colors in a Dreamweaver's loom, but such vibrant, unexpected colors! Surely that is something in which to rejoice." He met their eyes in turn; then he sighed. "But you have not told me what it is you need from me."

It was Karivet who found his voice and explained. Elgonar produced a bottle, filled it with water from the river in his house, and gave it into Karivet's keeping. Then he showed them to guest rooms where they could wash and rest. It felt wonderful to be warm and clean again. When they returned to the chamber with the Loom, Elgonar had laid a table with a simple meal of fish and stewed vegetables. They ate hungrily. Over the meal, the god told them that they could spend the night with him, but in the morning they would have to be on their way.

"I am grateful you have come," he told them, "for it has been too long since I have had people with whom to talk. But it would not be safe for you to remain with me longer

222

than a day and a night. My sister could make trouble for you. She jealously protects her territory, and although she will not trouble you while you quest, she would call it interference if I offered you aught beyond simple hospitality, and she would take steps. The only thing I can give you, besides the water, is some advice. My sister is cruel; she will cheat you if you are not on your guard, and that would be a pity after all your struggles. Walk warily with her and weigh her words carefully."

As he finished, Ychass looked up and met his eyes. "Purple is the Trickster's color, is it not?"

Elgonar hunched one shoulder. "It has been so in the past, when it has served her purpose. Truly, child of the Changing People, I dare tell you no more — only have courage, and remember, not all the gods are faithless." With that he rose from the table, excused himself, and left them to their own devices.

After their meal they went to their rooms, where each enjoyed the first truly restful night of their travels. They woke to a morning bright with sunlight. Though Elgonar had left a table set with a lavish breakfast, they saw no sign of him. They lingered over their meal in the hope that he would appear, but when he did not, they had to leave without thanking him again. The sun warmed their spirits as well as their bodies. Even the treacherous descent could not daunt them, and they turned their steps toward Windsmeet with light hearts.

TWENTY-ONE

 The trek out of the mountains was tiring but without incident. The companions reached the gentler foothills, and finally the plains, without confronting shapeshifters. Zan suspected that many of the high-circling hawks were sentries set to make sure she and the others did not stray from the riverbank, but she kept such thoughts to herself.

When at last it was time for them to leave the Snowsblood and head again into the dry lands, they spent a whole day resting by the river so that they would be fresh for the evening's travel. As the day drew to a close, they filled their water skins, settled their robes and packs comfortably, and made for the desert. They had grown unused to the shifting footing of the sands, and by the time they reached the spring at the knees of Windsmeet, they were footsore and weary. Zan dropped down beside the spring and drank thirstily.

"I think I'm too tired to eat," she said.

"Good. That will conserve our stores."

The unfamiliar voice made Zan start. She turned to find the point of a sword held steadily in her face. Her darting gaze took in that the others were similarly threatened, but there was no sign of Ychass. *Ychass?* She sent her mind questing.

A fly, Ychass replied. *With Iobeh. I will do what I can.*

"We have a quest to discharge," Zan said with all the bravado she could muster. "Do you dare risk the anger of the gods?"

"Rather that than the certain wrath of the Lord of the City," the Khedatheh retorted dryly. "Will you come quietly, then?"

Before Zan could answer, Remarr spoke harshly. "For shame, Edevvi! You call yourself Khedatheh, but you have forgotten the honor by which your people live. Even I, who carry no sword and make no pretense of valor or honor, know that it is the act of a scoundrel to take captive people under Khedathi protection without first offering *khed-harevel.*"

With foreboding, Zan took the meaning of the term from Edevvi's mind: trial by sword. Edevvi laughed. "What? *You've* found courage after all these years? Do you think to borrow a sword, or are you counting on the gods to preserve you? But your point is taken. We offer you challenge."

Vihena drew her sword, knocking aside the blade of the startled person who guarded her, and stepped to Remarr's side. "I am the Khedatheh here — of clan Khesst. I will meet your champion, for all that your challenge was made without courtesy." She was closely veiled and hooded, and in the uncertain light it was difficult to see her eyes. Edevvi's startled thought, *A Khesst! Gods!* was clear to Zan.

Edevvi stepped back with a slight bow, then with a gesture summoned the others. The guards sheathed their weapons and left the companions to gather in a tight knot and confer.

Remarr whispered to Vihena, "I didn't mean for you —"

She cut him off with a wave of one hand. *Sign. Voices carry. It was quick thinking. Don't apologize.*

You have friends among the garrison. I didn't mean —

Again she cut him off. *What do you think the Lord of the City wants with us? Those who sell their honor cannot afford friendship. Besides, I was never close to Edevvi. Where's Ychass?*

Near, Zan signed. *She will aid us if —*

No! Vihena's gesture was vehement. *This must be done with honor. If she chooses, she may flee, but any other action is treachery, and I will have no part of it.*

Ychass took her own shape in their midst. *I have no intention of abandoning you, you stiff-necked Khedatheh,* she signed to Vihena. *I have begun to understand friendship,* she thought to Zan, *but honor still baffles me.*

Me, too, Zan agreed feelingly.

"We have chosen our champion," one of the Tame Khedathi called, "if you are ready."

Vihena hesitated for a moment, then clapped Iobeh and Karivet's shoulders and met Zan's eyes. "If I fail, go peacefully." Then she turned to meet her challenger.

The two robed figures saluted one another, then closed, their swords clashing viciously. Zan tried to listen to their

226

thoughts as they fought, but their minds were full of the hiss and shiver of their weapons. Around and around they circled, swords darting, feet shifting quickly and surely. To Zan's untrained eye, their movements were graceful, like a beautiful, intricate dance, not a life-and-death struggle. She could not tell who was the more skillful; after a time, she could not even tell which was Vihena. It was easy to forget the two were fighting, until a sword found a mark and a dark stain bloomed on one combatant's upper arm, but only a sharp hiss of pain interrupted the circling. Their movements never slowed. Time was suspended. Zan was unready for the end when it came: a leap and a lunge, and a sword sliding cleanly into the other combatant's breast. The person left standing knelt and unhooked the fallen one's veil. The woman's eyelids fluttered weakly.

"Well fought, Vihena Khesst," she whispered. "I taught you well." The eyes closed.

"Khehaddi," Vihena said. Then her voice rose to a wail. "*Khehaddi!*" She reached to the throat of her own robes and rent them with a sharp yank. Then she buried her face in the dead captain's robes, her shoulders shaking.

The Tame Khedathi exchanged looks. "*Vihena,*" Edevvi hissed. "But she called herself Khesst!"

"And so she is," Remarr insisted. "Foster daughter to Emirri, leader of clan Khesst."

Edevvi stared at them all for a long moment. Then her control broke. "It's your doing," she cried, pointing at Zan. "What are you? Wonders happen in your wake. Orathi leave their forest and go questing, outcasts are accepted, a shapeshifter shows loyalty, and a City wench kills the greatest swordswoman of our age. Why?" In her anger, she grabbed Karivet by the shoulders and shook him until he met her eyes. "She doesn't belong here. Why has she come to trouble us?"

Karivet's voice went lifeless. "The Weaver strung her color on the Loom of Fate. What choice had she but to come? As for troubling you, it takes many influences to shape Fate's pattern. None of you is blameless in it."

"How *dare* you?" she raged.

"The oracle has no choice but to answer when questioned."

"Then answer this," Edevvi demanded, her voice trembling. "Vihena could never have won against Khehaddi in a fair fight. Why did my captain lose?"

"She permitted Vihena to win because she could not bear to see her die."

"Gods!" Edevvi gasped, and Vihena moaned in anguish. Karivet wrenched himself out of the stunned Khedatheh's grip. She stared at him with loathing. "You shouldn't have told me that," she said brokenly. "I didn't want to know."

"Then you shouldn't have asked me," Karivet told her, his face tight. "I answer what I am asked. I have no choice."

Edevvi wasn't listening. "To throw a fight like that — it's worse than lying. She's betrayed her honor; our honor demands that we cast her out. Now we can't even give her the rites of the dead. Her name will never be sung before the gods, and her spirit will wander homeless until the stars fall, and it's all because of you. *You!*" She pointed at Karivet.

"You *asked* me! I had no choice!"

Edevvi turned away without speaking. Silently the other Khedathi gathered their animals and gear. One of them caught the bridle of Khehaddi's horse and led it away. Then, without looking back at their fallen leader, they rode off into the morning light.

Zan, Ychass, and Iobeh set up the tent. No one spoke. Vihena would not leave Khehaddi's body, nor would she let anyone see to her wounded arm. Karivet sat apart from the others, huddled in misery. When Iobeh went to comfort him, he flinched away from her touch. As the silence deepened, Zan approvingly noted Iobeh's intent face. The tension eased away, and finally they slept.

When the camp roused, late in the afternoon, Zan found that Vihena had allowed Iobeh to wash and dress her wound. As Ychass and Zan cooked supper, Remarr tuned his harp and began to sing. It took Zan several minutes to realize he was singing about Khehaddi. The form of the song and much of the language seemed strangely archaic to her, and she was puzzled until Ychass explained. *It's the song for the dead,* she informed Zan. *Remarr is giving Khehaddi's name to the gods.*

As the last note of the song died into stillness, Vihena began to speak. "She was more than sister to me, more than mother. She accepted me; she didn't mock my interest as the passing fancy of a foolish Vematheh hoyden. She taught me, and she made the others accept me, too. She was a hundred times my master at the sword — I could never have beaten her, except that she let me. And I never once suspected it was she. She fought like Edevvi. Edevvi does everything impul-

229

sively; it is not a trait that improves her swordplay, though she is competent. Khehaddi gave me the opening Edevvi might have, and I took it, because I was weakening. I killed her. And all the time I thought she was Edevvi — as she meant me to. I *killed* her, and I would have died myself before I spilled Khehaddi's blood." Her voice broke.

For a moment no one spoke, then Ychass lifted her head. "She knew that," the shapeshifter said quietly, "and she felt the same way about you. Grieve for her, Vihena, but do not feel guilt. What she did, she did for you. It is a gift."

"But I don't want it, not at that cost. Ychass, she forfeited her *honor*."

"No." It was Remarr who spoke. "No, Vihena, she did not. She forfeited her honor when she sold it to the City. With what she did for you, she took it back." He raised one empty hand, closed it into a fist, and drew it toward himself.

Vihena was silent for a moment, then she met his eyes. "And so you gave her name to the gods."

Remarr held her gaze. "I did. And in the morning I will help you bury her. She was a brave woman, one who followed her heart in what was important."

Vihena nodded, then managed a weak smile. "For one who claims no honor of his own, you understand a great deal, Minstrel Remarr, and I thank you."

After that they lapsed into silence, but the tension was gone. They ate their meal, banked the fire, and set out for Windsmeet to confront the god.

TWENTY-TWO

 *The shuttle hissed through the warp. Ei-koheh impatiently pushed back a way-ward strand of hair and sighed.*

"Tired?" *Ohmiden asked.*

"I have never been more weary, but we're nearly at the end. This night's work should allow me to bring the pattern full circle. I can't say I'll be sorry to lay my shuttle down."

Ohmiden nodded. He saw how worn the weaver's face was.

"Though truthfully, I won't rest easy until I hear their footsteps on the stoop and see their faces. I —" Suddenly her face drained of color. "No!" she gasped. The shuttle strug-gled in her hands like a live thing, and she fought with it while the sweat beaded on her brow. Ohmiden watched helplessly, fearful of breaking the weaver's fragile control.

"Dear gods!" she cried out. "I'm losing it. Quick, Ohmi-den — gray! I need the gray wool."

*

The companions reached the scoured top of Windsmeet just as the moon was rising. Zan stood watching the flat silver disk clear the horizon while Karivet called out to summon the god. His cry ended and the world settled back to stillness. Then there was a skirl of wind and dust and the god stood before them.

"You have returned," she greeted them. "Did you bring me what I requested?"

Silently Karivet handed her the bottle Elgonar had given them. She studied it for a moment, then, with a peculiar laugh, she drew the cork and upended the bottle. The water's splash against the rock was loud in the silence. They stared at her in shock.

"You should see your faces," the god mocked them. "You can't understand why I would spill out that which has taken you weeks to gain. It cost you hardships and danger, and I spill it wastefully on the thirsty rock. You want to know why. Well, I'll tell you. Your toil, your hardships, your time, your very lives — none of them has any value for me. I sent you after the snows' blood because it amused me to do so. So ask your boon — perhaps your privations have made you wise enough to ask well."

Karivet raised his head. "We had thought to ask for justice, but I think it would be better if we were more specific. Lady, we came here in order to ask the gods for a decree that will keep the Vemathi and their Khedathi servants from taking Orathi lands. Will you grant us such?"

The god considered. Finally she nodded. "If they are minded to heed my words, I will give you such a decree. But now, you have toiled hard and amused me tolerably well. You must permit me to reward you."

Zan, prompted by an inner squirm of unease, spoke up. "Lady, your gracious decree is all the reward we seek."

She laughed merrily. "That will make this unexpected boon all the sweeter."

"We do not wish to trouble you unduly," Remarr added.

"Why, you have already done that by asking for a decree — unless you've changed your mind and no longer want it? No? Well, in that case, you must permit me to reward you. I insist." There was ice in her tone. When they were all silent, the god drew her breath in sharply. "If I thought there was anything more than simple ignorance behind your rudeness, I would immediately rescind my boon to you. One would think you'd been warned against my generosity — which we all know simply could *not* be the case. The proper response to a god who offers you a boon is 'Yes, thank you very much, gracious Lady.' Now, would you like that decree, children?"

"Yes, thank you very much, gracious Lady," they chorused obediently.

"And you will permit me to reward you? Consider: you may not have one boon without the other. I am determined in this."

They exchanged looks. All their doubts were summed up in Iobeh's shrug. They didn't like it, but they had no choice. "Yes, thank you very much, gracious Lady." The chorus was more ragged this time.

"Oh, I'm so glad. I do *so* like to give gifts." Her smile sent fear crawling up Zan's spine. "But you didn't speak," she added to Iobeh.

"My sister is mute," Karivet told her.

"Ah. But you *do* want my gift? Nod."

Iobeh nodded miserably.

"Good. Then you're first. I will give you a voice, so that you may thank me properly." She frowned for a moment in concentration. "There you are — say thank you."

Iobeh had closed her eyes in a wince of momentary pain. Now she opened them wide with delight and gratitude. "Thank you."

For an instant everyone was stunned, then Iobeh clapped both hands over her mouth. The voice that had issued from her mouth was a hideous croak, a harsh mockery of speech. The others had recoiled instinctively. When Zan saw the hurt in Iobeh's eyes, she remembered that the girl could feel her reaction, the initial recoil. Zan fought down a wave of bitter fury at the god who had such a gift for cruelty, and concentrated instead on her love for Iobeh, but she knew the damage was done. The god looked around at them all, malicious amusement apparent in her eyes.

"It may not be the most mellifluous of voices," she said mockingly, "but surely it's better than *nothing*. Now, who's next?" She turned to Vihena. "Ah yes. Our Vematheh. It must have been such a trial to you, growing up without any beauty — you must have long since despaired of ever finding a husband. But I shall end all that for you." Her hands began moving in the air. "I will give you a face and a form men would die for. There. Now you no longer need hide behind a veil."

Zan's jaw dropped. Vihena was gorgeous; her face was prettier and more delicate even than her mother's, and her robes hung on her differently. But the beauty was marred by the anguish in her eyes. Suddenly Zan understood. Vihena had repudiated the Vemathi way. She had not let herself be raised to be an ornament in some merchant's household. Her waywardness had been permitted because she did not look the part; now that she so decidedly *did* look the part, there would be no more tolerance for her attitude. Zan touched her thoughts fleetingly. *She has made me a slave — or worse!* Zan gripped her wrist firmly. "You have a home in the desert," she whispered. "Clan Khesst will accept you no matter what face you wear behind your veil!" Vihena did not look greatly reassured, though some of the panic left her eyes.

The god turned to Remarr. "For you, courage." Her hand clenched slowly and Remarr winced. "There. Aren't you going to thank me?"

"No," he replied coolly. "Since you have given me courage — an utterly unnecessary attribute for a minstrel — I am going to tell you exactly what I think of you. You are cruel, small-minded, and malicious, and unfortunately you have the power to amuse yourself at our expense."

In answer the god raised one finger and pointed. A whip of violet lightning exploded in the minstrel's face. He dropped with a cry of pain and lay still. As Zan and Iobeh sprang to his side, the god remarked, "If he lives, he will have to learn that there are some drawbacks to courage — especially rash courage, which seems to be the sort I've given him. Now, the shapeshifter." She held Ychass's eyes for a long moment. Apparently the contact did not satisfy her, for when she broke the gaze, she was pouting. "To you I have given thoughts that can be heard by the thought-deaf."

"Thank you, Lady," Ychass said blandly. *I think I've escaped fairly lightly — and this new trick may even be useful, once I learn to control it.*

Iobeh, Karivet, and Vihena looked up, startled, and the god turned away in irritation.

"Now, the Orathen seer." Her smile curled cruelly. "To you, child, I will give the power of choice: you will be able to choose whether or not to answer a given question. Unfortunately, I cannot give you also the ability to know what you will say, for that would be a second gift, so your choice will always be made blind. But at least you will have the choice."

Karivet raised tormented eyes to the god's face, and she laughed. Zan heard his thoughts. *To have to choose, when the answer may be helpful or hurtful, or the question may even be wrong . . . It's easier when it just happens — then the prophecy isn't my fault, my responsibility.* Zan withdrew from his mind, at a loss. She could think of no comfort to offer him. Beside her, Remarr moaned and stirred.

"Oh, good," the god said. "He'll live. Now for you, Stranger. You're easy. I shall send you home."

Zan's heart constricted suddenly. She looked up at the god in desperation. "Home is a place in the heart," she said

236

through a tight throat, but when she tried to summon an image of Eikoheh's cottage, she found herself listening to her own voice saying, "Thanks to you, the only home I've ever known is Logan International Airport." She fought a sudden dizziness, a rushing in her ears. With her last shred of will she gasped, "Elgonar! Elgonar, help!" Then the world went dark.

"No!" *The weaver's scream shook the cottage.* "No!"

Before the second cry had ceased, Ohmiden was at her side. The shuttle was still in her hands, and it took him a moment to discover the cause of her distress, but when he saw, he gasped aloud. The strand of red that had been in the pattern from the beginning had disappeared at the end. It had not unraveled, but was broken off, its end dangling forlornly out of the cloth on the loom. He looked at Eikoheh in consternation. " 'Tsan?"

She nodded, tears trembling in her old eyes. "I've lost her."

"Dead?"

The weaver shook her head. "No. But gone. Gone as suddenly as she came."

"Perhaps she'll find her way back here. She came once, after all."

"Fool," *the old woman chided, without rancor.* "She was drawn into the Loom once — it was no accident, her coming."

"Well, then neither was her going. Let her go. Her task is done."

Eikoheh met his eyes levelly. "Ohmiden, I give you my dreams."

He suppressed a shudder at the ancient phrase.

"I felt her cry out as she was torn — torn — from the pattern. She did not go willingly."

The old man sighed. "Eikoheh, you must either let her go or weave her back — if you can."

The weaver nodded, gesturing with her chin to the spool of thread in her hands. Ohmiden's eyes widened as he realized that she meant to try. He watched her as she gathered the colors and began to reestablish control. She would rework the pattern into a larger framework. He watched the shuttle fly for a moment before he turned away with a silent sigh. He would make dinner; they needed to eat, after all.

The swirling darkness cleared into a searing white light that left Zan blinking. And the *noise*. Without thinking she clapped her hands to her ears, but even that didn't lessen the babble. She forced her eyes open. She was surrounded by people. Oddly dressed, they were milling around in front of her, dragging heavy-looking satchels — *suitcases*. With the word, the scene snapped into familiarity: an airport terminal. Cautiously she lowered her hands.

"Passengers from flight 216 from New York are now arriving at gate 21." It took concentration for Zan to make sense of the announcer's bored voice. She pressed one hand to her forehead. There was the thrum of a headache behind her eyes.

"Excuse me, miss. Are you all right?" *Damned doped-out religious lunatic.*

Zan blinked at the double-threaded message. A man in a uniform stood next to her. *Airport security,* some disused corner of her brain supplied. "Yes. Yes, I'm fine. Thank you," she replied, fighting a wave of nausea and trying to sound normal. It was hard to speak English after all this time. She wasn't sure she was intelligible, but after another close look, the man went away.

She leaned against the wall and closed her eyes. Summoning all the mental energy she could, she blanked others' thoughts out of her mind. She had to *think.* She felt for her pack, but no, she had left it in the camp. Besides, what use would that be to her *here?* She began to realize how very out of place she looked in her white desert robes. No wonder the security officer had reacted badly. She suppressed a groan as she realized that she had none of the necessities of survival: no identification, no money. How was she going to manage? She battled panic. The god had sent her home — *home!* — to strangers, squalor, and isolation.

She gathered all her mental energy again and sent her thought-voice shrieking outward: *Ychass! Elgonar! DON'T LEAVE ME HERE!* Strangers' thoughts intruded dizzyingly, but there was no response. Aching despair washed through her and she swallowed tears. Distractedly, she pushed her hood back. She was too warm in this close, damp air.

Suddenly she noticed the last thing she expected to find here: someone she knew. Rolly Castleman, her father's agent, was leaving the gate area ahead of her. She hesitated, trying to decide whether to hide or to approach him. She knew that she needed help, and that Rolly would certainly be capable of dealing with all the details, but he would ask her questions — and what could she say?

Before she made up her mind, he turned. His eyes flicked over her, then snapped back, widened.

"*Alexandra!*" He started toward her, his mouth already pursing for the first question. Zan's brain went into overdrive, searching for explanations, excuses, anything with which to mollify him. "Where on *earth* have you been?"

"Oh, Rolly," she gasped. "Thank *God* I've found you." Without any prompting from her, her chin began to quiver. "Oh, Rolly, you've got to help me!"

"Now relax, Zan. Of course I'll help you, but what's going on? What are you doing in that outlandish outfit? And *where the hell have you been for the past five months?*"

Five months? Zan thought. Had it been only five months? It seemed like years, at least. But she realized how long five months would seem to him — what an inexplicable absence. What on earth could she say to appease him? It had to be something he'd believe — and something she could be expected not to want to discuss. The answer sprang to mind, beautiful in its simplicity. She hid a smile in a tremulous tone. "The cult," she whispered. "I can't talk about it now, just get me out of here before they find me and take me back."

Rolly blinked at her, speechless for once. Then he took her arm. "You come along with me, Zan," he murmured soothingly. "I'll help you get things straightened out. You've clearly had a bad time of it, but we'll get everything worked out. Everything is going to be just fine, Zan, you'll see."